MAFIA, LLC

THE CONTI STORY CONTINUES

Other Books by Paul Tripi

The Right Hand of the Father

Roses are White, The Conti Story

Untamed Rivers

MAFIA, LLC

THE CONTI STORY CONTINUES

Paul Tripi

This book is copyrighted by Paul Tripi

No part of this book may be used or copied without the written permission of the copyright holder.

2020

This is a book of fiction. All places, characters and circumstances are products of the author's imagination, or if real, are used in a fictitious manner.

MAFIA, LLC

THE CONTI STORY CONTINUES

By Paul Tripi

Chapter 1
The Prologue *

* Chapter One, The Prologue, is a recap taken from the book "Roses are White- The Conti Story" which preceded this novel.

Peter Conti sat in the office of his newly acquired restaurant, the Delaware Grill replaying all the circumstances that got him to this point in life. How did an All-American kid from the suburbs become the leader of one of the families of the most infamous crime syndicate in the world, the Mafia. Thoughts were resonating though his mind on just how he became The Don, The Man, **THE GODFATHER**. Peter Conti just sat there reminiscing.

Jacqueline Millen
(Love at First Sight)

He met his wife, Jacqueline Millen Conti, when he was nine years old. He fell in love with her in the fourth grade. She felt the same way. Back then it was puppy love, but their feelings continued to develop and over the years grew to the point that by high school it was a torrid love affair. She was the one, period!

The long wait for the two to finally become a couple happened at a house party.

Peter was good at everything. He lettered in three sports. He was quarterback of the football team, starting guard on the basketball team, and star third baseman on the baseball team. He was an "A" student and was liked by all, nice resume for an 18-year-old kid without a worry in the world. That is except how he can get the one thing he wanted most out of life, a date with Jackie.

"Hey asshole," said Sonny, Peter's best friend, as he walked up behind Pete at his locker.

"I hope you're not talking to me," replied Peter

"Is there some other gutless guy, standing at your locker, drooling over a girl 7 lockers away, who doesn't have the balls to ask her out?" asked his buddy.

"I've got plenty of balls. You wanna see um?" answered Peter.

"Gross, you're disgusting," replied Sonny with a look on his face like he just bit into a lemon.

"Thanks for the compliment. Now what do you want?" asked Peter.

"Party over at Rosey's house Friday night. Why don't you show some of those balls of yours, figuratively speaking of course, and walk over there and ask Jackie to go with you?"

"Cause it would be like asking my sister to go out. We're just too good of friends to ruin it by dating. You know that."

"I know that you're good enough friends to talk to her about it. Ya know she might just be feeling the same way about you. Smarten up."

"God, Sonny, I wish that were true."

"You're stupid! What do you have to lose?"

"How about the best friend of my life, that's what," replied Peter.

"What am I, chopped liver?"

"Well, actually, you kind of smell like it."

"That crazy Rosey challenged me to eat 4 Big Herby burgers," responded Sonny.

"And, of course, you did."

"That's why I smell a little, you know, gas," blurted out Sonny.

"Oh, you sick bastard—I just threw up in my mouth a little, get away from me, I mean it," said Peter making a face like he was going to puke.

"I gotta go anyway. I'm making myself sick. That woman is going to kill me one day."

"You can say NO to your girlfriend sometime, you know, Jesus Sonny, really, GET AWAY FROM ME NOW," yelled Peter.

Rosey's party went great. It seemed like everyone was having a blast, everyone but Peter that is. Jackie was there with Ronnie Atom. A nice enough guy who thought he was way cooler than he really was. Peter had enough of watching Jackie dance with the guy and decided it was time for him to leave. After he danced a dance or two, with one of the girls from the small covey of unaccompanied gals gathered by the punch bowl, he said his goodbyes and was getting ready to take off.

As he was walking out, Peter noticed a little tiff going on between Jackie and Ronnie. He watched for a second and started drifting over to let's say eavesdrop a might. He didn't get close enough to hear what the tiff was about because, before he was in range, Ronnie had grabbed Jackie by her arm. She was seriously trying to pull herself away when she was assisted by "guess who?" Peter punched Ron so hard in the forehead he hit the ground like a turf falling from a tall horse. As he laid there, with Peter standing over him, he heard, "Now you can get up and try to defend yourself, but all you'll get for your trouble is the beating of your life, try me," said Peter with a look on his face that definitely said he meant business.

"If you ever lay a hand on Jackie again, I won't just beat the shit out of you, I'll kill you. Is that clear enough."

"Is that supposed to be some kind of a threat?" answered Ronnie with absolutely no thought of getting up.

"No Ronnie, that's not a threat, that's a promise!"

As the young pugilist turned to see if Jackie was all right, he felt her arms wrap around him.

"Oh my God Peter!"

"What happened?" he said as he turned back towards Ronnie with full intensions of finishing something he just started.

Jackie grabbed Peter as he turned, stopped him and said, "Nothing, it's over now."

"What's over? What happened? What the hell did he do?"

"It's not what he did, it's what he wanted to do," she said holding his arm knowing what was about to happen next if she didn't.

There was no power on earth that could have stopped Peter Conti as he pulled his arm from Jackie's grasp and turned to look for the already disappearing foe, except Jackie.

"Peter, Please. Will you just stay with me a minute and hold me?"

"Of course," he whispered as he held her head against his chest. "I'll hold you for the rest of our lives."

She looked up at him and kissed him like a woman would kiss her man that was going off to war. No words were said for a minute or two. They just stood there holding each other.

"Peter" she said softly, "You are the most"

"Stop," he said interrupting her, "Don't say something you might regret."

"Regret, I've regretted not saying this to you for years. Are you going to make me say the words?"

"No Jackie, "No need. But there is something I need to say to you."

She put her fingers over his mouth and kissed him again.

The next night would be their first official date. The date they both had waited almost a decade for.

THE DATE

When Jacqueline Millen walked into Jakes, the official bar every student of age from Tonawanda Senior High frequented, she was a vision of grandeur. She was absolutely breathtaking. Dressed to the nines and made up like she was posing for Glamour Magazine. She was trying to look the best that she could, and her mission was accomplished.

Peter looked up from his chair and almost fell out of it. It's funny how someone can look at another person for 10 years and really never see them. But that particular moment, seeing Jackie and really looking at her, would stay in Peter's memory banks for the rest of his life.

"Jesus, Mary, and Joseph," Peter whispered to himself.

"Jackie, you look simply beautiful!" he said so loud the whole place could hear him.

"Thank you, kindly sir," she replied with a curtsy.

"I'd better. I've been working on this look for an hour," she said smiling with a smile that was so bright she looked like she was doing a toothpaste commercial.

"I'm meeting someone here. Do you want to wait with me?" she added.

"What do you mean? What are you talking about? Who?" replied a semi-confused Peter?

"Oh, you. I've been waiting what seems like forever for you to ask me out and you have the audacity to ask, who, Peter Conti, for being one of the smartest guys I know, you sure are dumb."

"I was stupefied by your beauty," he replied. "Did that make up for it?"

"In spades," she answered.

"You don't look so bad yourself," she added.

"Thanks," he replied. "I took a shower yesterday, just because I knew we were going out. I didn't change my underwear though. No sense in spoiling you."

Jackie just laughed and laughed. She sat down at the table and ordered a Coke. She was just shy of her 18th birthday, too young to drink, but it didn't matter, alcohol wasn't her thing.

"What would you like to do tonight?" he asked.

"Can we just talk for awhile?" she replied.

"Of course. Your wish is my command. You can have what ever you want whenever you want it for the rest of our lives. Jackie Millen, I'm head over heals in love with you! I don't know what will happen from here, but I do know I would hate myself for the rest of my life if I let life slip by without saying that to you."

Jackie hesitated a second, smiled, and replied, "I knew you were slow, but I didn't think you were blind. There has never been another boy for me. I never thought for a minute that we wouldn't be together, forever. You are the love of my life. I came here with the same thought. If this night ends with us going our separate way, at least I would have gotten a chance to tell you that I love you, and that I have loved you what seems like forever!"

Peter squeezed even harder on Jackie's hand, not a word was said for what seemed like an hour, but it was only a minute or two. A single tear fell from Jackie's eye before Peter broke the silence and said, "Just remember who said it first."

College
(The Scholarship)

The love they had for each other was lifelong. Peter was a perfect male specimen in every way. He was a magnificent high school athlete and had numerous scholarships to the most prestigious colleges in America, until a severe sports related injury ended that opportunity.

"Peter! You got a letter from SUNY (State University of New York)," Yelled Peter's mom Theresa as she opened the mail.

"Hell, Mom they don't even have a damn football team," he answered.

"Watch you mouth."

"Sorry Mom," he said as he grabbed his letter and walked into the living room to read it.

"What does it say?" she asked inquisitively.

"Well, I'll be. Mom, you are not going to believe this!"

"What? Believe What?"

"It says here, the State University of New York at Buffalo has approved your request for an academic scholarship and are awarding you, Peter Conti, a scholarship which includes tuition and books for as long as you keep a 3.5 GPA. This award is good for the school years starting August 1966 and lasting until August 1970. For further information, contact the Admissions Office at 1700 Elmwood Avenue, Buffalo, New York   Congratulations!"

"Oh my God! Thomas, Thomas," Theresa shouted out the back door to her husband who was cleaning the garage.

"WHAT---I'M BUSY?" he yelled.

"Come here quick."

Thomas Conti darted into the kitchen expecting to see a fire or something. When he didn't see any apparent danger he quickly said, "Jesus Christ Theresa what's so damn important that you screamed like the house was on fire."

"Peter just received a letter from Buffalo State. He got a free ride. A scholastic scholarship isn't that just unbelievable."

"How?"

Just as he got that word out, Jackie came running in from her house just around the corner. Peter had called her just moments after finding out for himself.

"I can't believe it!" she exclaimed. "I just sent in the request a month ago."

"You sent in the request?" said Peter.

"Yes!! You think the only reason people get scholarships is because they can throw something real far? You're brilliant, you idiot. For crying out loud you've never even gotten a B in your life."

"You're right I am exstreming intelagrent ain't I," he jokingly answered.

"Yes, you are, and, if you plan on keeping your promise to me, I need you to have that college degree we've been counting on."

"Wait a minute. MOM. Jackie's trying to marry me again," he yelled out as he covered his head with his shoulder to protect against the expected punch in the arm.

"You keep up the good work Jackie and one of these times he'll realize that that might just be a good idea," she said as she slapped him on the same shoulder as Jackie.

"Honey, why didn't you tell us about this. It's so wonderful. Thank you so much". Peter's dad said as he hugged Jackie tightly.

"I'd marry you myself if I hadn't made the terrible mistake of marrying Theresa," Tom said raising his shoulder waiting for the same slap. That of course came.

"But thank you sweetheart. We didn't know HOW we were going to come up with the money to get this idiot to go to college. This is an answer to our prayers."

"Thank you all but it was Mr. Miller who deserves the credit. He was asking me about Peter's health after the accident and I told him what was going on. You know, about the offers being rescinded for the scholarships and all. He's the one who told me what Peter should do. I just skipped a step and did it myself. Mr. Miller gave me Peter's transcripts saying he would need them for applications. He's really sorry how everything worked out. He said he is Peter's biggest fan. No big deal."

"No big deal???" Peter said grabbing her.

"Thank you, thank you, thank you!!" and he kissed her full on the mouth right in front of his parents. Something Peter would normally never do.

"Wow, that was worth it. Now, I expect you to wash my car every week for a year."

"No problem said Peter's mom. Of course, I'll do it."

"I was talking to Peter Mrs. Conti."

"I know, I just said that for fun. Now you go over there right now Peter and wash this girl's car."

Everybody laughed. But what just happened was a miracle as far as the Conti family was concerned. The Contis, by the way, have included Jackie as part of the family for a long time.

Sonny, Ray, and Al

(The Friends)
and
(The Sports Injury)

Peter had many friends, but three that were as close as brothers to him. Peter was sure they would be in his life forever. The four of them were inseparable and grew from boys to men together. They were part of each other's lives in every way, shape, and form.

Saturday's baseball playoff game was between Tonawanda and Kenmore East at their field. It was a big game for both teams. The winner would go on to the regionals, while the loser would stay home and watch. Their season would be over.

Jackie led the possession of cheerleaders to the front of the stands as they started their chants. Of course, Jackie was a cheerleader. How could they be the perfect couple without that? It just seemed like nothing could go wrong in the blessed lives of these two young adults. Then it happened.

Bottom of the 6th, Tonawanda was leading by 2 but Kenmore was up, and they had the bases loaded with only 1 out. THS had taken the lead on Peter's double in the gap with two outs in the fifth. Ray was pitching a great game, but he was getting the ball a little up that inning and the Kenmore guys were taking advantage of it. Ray had a worried look on his face as he rubbed up the ball getting ready for his next pitch. Peter noticing the anxiety on his buddy's face, called time out, and went to the mound.

"Ray, you've been pitching your whole life and you're good. Real good. Remember that when you throw this next pitch. This guy can't hit you buddy. One more thing, you've got 8 other guys out here behind you. If he gets lucky and does hit it, we'll catch it. Now do your thing man. No worries buddy."

The next pitch came; swing, and the Kenmore batter hit a high foul ball along the third base side. Peter turned and ran back as fast as his legs could carry him. The ball was coming down over his left shoulder and he had his eyes on it all the way. Just as the ball hit his glove, he stumbled over a rut close to the brick wall that ran along the left field sideline and flew headfirst into the structure. Peter went black.

When he woke up, he was in Kenmore Mercy Hospital. He was totally disoriented and scared. The only people in the room were his mother, his father, and Jackie. Jackie and Theresa were crying in each other's arms and Tom stood standing in the corner trying not to cry, but it wasn't working. Peter tried to gather his thoughts but couldn't seem to place what was going on. He tried to speak but he couldn't. Three times he tried to call out but nothing. Finally, he spurted out the word, "Mom."

Theresa scrambled to her son's side. Reaching out for his hand in a panic she grabbed it and said, "Oh, thank you Jesus. Thank you, Jesus, !!"

Peter wanted to ask a bunch of questions but couldn't. Only his eyes could ask. His mother still crying started answering the unasked questions.

"You're in the hospital honey." she choked out. "You've been out for 2 days." She tried to continue but couldn't.

His father standing over his wife's shoulder, tears still running down his face continued.

"You were in a coma son," he said with his tears of fear turning to tears of joy. "We didn't know if we were going to lose you," he said, gathering himself so as not to scare his son anymore than he already had.

But Theresa was doing quite well at accomplishing that feat all by herself. Her tears of joy were loud and uncontrollable.

"Honey, Please, Peter needs you strong now. Come up here and talk with us."

Jackie dashed into the room, followed closely by the Peter's doctor. All three stood behind him as he examined Peter using some instrument that allowed him to peer deep into Peter's eyes.

"Well Doctor?" asked Tom Conti almost pleadingly, "Is he all right?"

"Too soon to tell now Mr. Conti. Your son has had major trauma to his brain. The fact that he even woke up after surgery is all we could have hoped for thus far. Right now, he needs plenty of rest and close observation. He's going to be here awhile."

Again, Theresa Conti started to cry but this time she wasn't sure why. Just the unknown was getting to her. The entire time the doctor was speaking Jackie sat in a chair in the corner of the room and wept.

Three days passed and Peter was starting to focus much better. His speech was not impaired and his physical condition, along with his appetite, were well on their way to where they were before the collision with the wall. His family almost never left his side the entire time. There was always someone there with him, be it his mother, father, or Jackie. Now that he was on his way to getting his strength back, friends were allowed to visit.

As much as Sonny, Ray, and Al wanted to pimp their buddy, calling him a pussy and slacker and whatever else they could think of just to avoid saying their true feeling, it didn't work. All three lifelong friends were worried sick for days and when they finally saw their buddy, joking and name calling just didn't seem to fit. Peter's eyes were blackened. The left side of his head was still swollen from the incision the doctors had to make to relieve the swelling in his brain. He looked like 5 miles of ruff road.

"Jesus Peter, are you alright?" They all said almost in unison.

"You ought to see the other guy," he said with a smile that was obviously a little painful.

"What can we do man? Just name it," asked Al, almost whispering.

"There is nothing you guys can do. I just need time to heal. I have what they call a cerebral concussion and there's no fixing it."

"What does that mean?" asked Sonny obviously worried as hell.

"It means that when I hit the wall part of my brain detached from my skull. It's gonna be detached, maybe forever."

"Wait, explain that a little more. What do you mean forever," asked Sonny.

"No problem guys. Everything will be back to normal pretty soon. It just means I'll be getting some pretty bad headaches every now and again."

"Bad ones?" asked Ray quietly.

"Not good ones Ray. I've had a few already and they kind of make you sick to your stomach," answered Pete trying not to make it sound worse than it is.

"Hey guys, no one told me. Did we win the game?"

"Yeah, we won. They tied it up in the sixth, but our buddy Ray here hit a dinger over the right field wall in the seventh. We won 3 to 2," answered Sonny.

"I don't know how he even saw the ball. He was crying like a girl at the plate," inserted Al.

"I wasn't crying!! Dirt flew into my eyes," replied Ray emphatically. Then he leaned over to Peter and whispered, "No fucking way we were going to lose that game after they carried you off that field. No fucking way!!"

"You did pitch a hell of a game Ray. A hell of a game!!" Sonny said defending his friend.

"Yeah, you were great Ray," said Al. "I'm only giving you shit. You were great. I could barely see you anyway, I was crying myself. Same dirt."

"How long before you're back? Did the Doctor say," asked Sonny.

"Well, that's the good news. You guys aren't gonna have to waste your time watching me play any college games. I'm gonna be normal in every way except there will be no more contact sports for me, can't take another hit to the head. I guess I'll go to college, but not on a scholarship."

The 3 friends just stood there. Not a word was said. Their hero, the best damn athlete they had ever seen in their short lives was done.

"You're gonna be all right, that's all that matters. Fuck sports. All they do is make you sweat and smell like Al," said Sonny doing his best to break the tension of the worst news they've ever heard.

"Fuck Sports? Fuck Sports?" answered Pete. "Haven't you guys ever heard of GOLF!!!"

Vito Bansano
(The Meeting)

Peter met Vito Bansano at a restaurant he would stop at for dinner each night when traveling between work and college.

Vito owned the restaurant Peter frequented, named The Delaware Grill. Vito noticed and respected the boy's character and polite attitude and on one of the occasions introduced himself.

He quickly realized Peter had no idea of his title or of the underlining purpose of the restaurant. Vito was comfortable with Peter and soon joined him for dinner often. Peter was like a sponge listening to Vito's stories about the old country. Vito was born in the same town in Italy as Peter's grandparents. Peter relished the conversations. He was proud of his Italian heritage and it showed. They soon became friends, good friends. Peter showed the old man respect every minute they were together, and Vito loved the fact that the kid did so without knowing what his "other" job was. Their relationship was enjoyable to Vito. It was comfortable and calming to this man, and Vito, who was childless, grew attached to the young man. They were friends.

Their talks went on for a long while and then one day Vito said, "Peter, I don't think you should come here anymore. Don't ask me why. You don't want to know. Just know that, if you ever need anything, anything at all, you come to me. You have made a friend and I am a good friend to have. Capisci?"

"Yes sir, I understand. I'll miss you though," is all Peter said. He kind of knew all along that Vito was probably involved in other businesses. He dressed like he was the president of the United States and everyone around him treated him with unbelievable respect and that fact was obviously noticeable. Vito always excused himself when talking to people when Peter was present; he never let Peter hear any conversations.

Peter finished his last meal at the Delaware Grill, a veal parmesan sandwich and started to walk out. He stopped, walked over to Vito, and stuck out his hand. He leaned over and, as a sign of respect kissed the man on his cheek.

"Goodbye sir."

"Goodbye **my young friend**."

Little did Peter know what kind of turn of events would transpire over that friendship. Nobody could have. Peter Conti, all American boy and Vito Bansano, also known as The Don, the Head Man, Numero Uno, the Boss who was respectfully referred to by all made men, (soldiers who were members of the Italian Mafia) as the GODFATHER.

SElective Service

(The Army Draft)

It was 1969 and the war in Vietnam was raging. The Untied States was in need of more fighting men. There was a draft. A lottery system went into effect and all eligible men over the age of 18 were placed into a drawing. A pill was drawn from two bins: one bin held days of the year and one had numbers from 1 thru 366, including leap year. They pulled a date, which were birth dates, and then a number. If the number attached to a given birth date was less than 120, the young man was going to be drafted into the military. If the number was between 120 and 180, the odds were good that the person would not be drafted. If the number was greater than 180 the individual would not be needed. Peter drew number 7. **Hello Uncle Sam.**

Army Training Camp

(Boot Camp)

Peter, as mentioned, was good at everything. He was also well prepared for what he was going to go through at boot camp. His father, a WWII veteran, helped prepare Peter for the ordeal. Peter was ready for whatever they were going to throw at him.

Private first class (PFC) Peter Conti's platoon, 1st Platoon was at the top of the list in almost every training competition and for one reason, or should I say one person.

First came the rifle range. Best shot in the entire camp, PFC Peter Conti 1st Platoon.
Next came the mile run, te fastest runner on the base, PFC Peter Conti 1st Platoon.
Obstacle course, best time, that's right, PFC Peter Conti 1st Platoon.
Obstacle coarse, best accumulated time, 1st Platoon, Peter Conti Platoon leader.

And it went that way for 13 weeks. If Peter didn't win the contest he was near the top. When graduation day came around, all the guys were trying to figure out where they would be heading when Sergeant Riker came into the barracks and yelled,

"Conti, front and center."

"Yes Sergeant," he yelled.

"Follow me Conti, the Major wants to see you"

Peter had no idea what was going on. He hadn't done a single thing wrong and had followed every rule to the letter of the law.

"Wait here Conti."

Sergeant Robert Riker walked into the Major's office with Peter just outside.

"Are you sure about this boy Bob?" asked the Major.

"Yes sir, dead sure, I'll stake my reputation on him. He's diligent, intelligent, and a born leader. He can shoot the eye out of a snake at 1000 yards, cook it up, and make it taste like lobster. He's fast, strong, toughest guy in the camp, and fearless. Sir I'd be honored to fight side by side with this man. He's the best I've ever had."

"That's high praise coming from a soldier like you Bob. Send the man in."

Peter walked into the Majors office saluted and stood at attention.

"At ease soldier." The Major hesitated for a second or two and said, "Private Conti, your record and accomplishments during training camp have been exemplary. Soldier, we have a unit for men like you, men who show unusual skills, courage, and special abilities. It will mean additional training, but when you have completed that training you will be part of the most elite, most feared fighting force, this man's army can offer, Special Forces, son. Welcome to the GREEN BARETS."

Riker stood in the corner wearing a smile. He was proud of what Peter was able to accomplish and he hoped that he had some small part of making him the soldier he turned out to be. As they walked out of the Major's office, Riker told Peter how he felt,

"Congratulation Soldier. You deserve this. If there is anything, I can do for you, you let me know. I said this behind your back and now I say it to you face. I'd be proud to fight beside you Pete. Good Luck," he said, as the two men shook hands.

Peter was honored. Once you go through basic training, all the information and conversations you've had with the civilian population become moot. All the, be careful, don't volunteer for anything, and don't be a hero advice goes by the wayside. You're a soldier. You do your duty to the best of your ability. Your reason for living, your purpose, is to defend your county and all the people who live in it. At that exact moment, with the Major's words still ringing in his head, Peter knew what his duty was. He was going to train and learn everything he possibly could. He was going to heed his father's words and "BE THE BEST THAT HE COULD BE." Peter Conti was going to become one lean, mean, KILLING MACHINE.

Special Forces/Green Beret
(Training)

Special Forces training was intense and then some. You were taught how to fire every kind of weapon the army had to offer and fire it on target. Not just the standard M-14, which had a limited range, but assault rifles that could kill a man from 2,000 yards. That's over a mile away. They were taught numerous ways to kill a man with their hands, their feet, their fingers, their thumbs, knives, bayonets, rocks, and ropes. Hell, they were taught 20 ways to kill a man with a spoon. They learned to disarm, disable, and dismember the enemy. They became fearsome soldiers, with the skills to go on missions in small forces and get the job done. Even if the force was one person.

Their physical training wasn't any picnic either. There were numerous parachute jumps. Being in the airborne division was a prerequisite to being a Green Beret. No, that was like falling out of bed for these guys. But being dropped out of a helicopter in the middle of the Everglades with nothing but a knife and a compass and expected to meet up with their comrades in a certain number of days, now that takes some skills. Brass balls too. After that was accomplished, they were dropped in the dessert with the same equipment and a small amount of water with the same orders. Their next assignment required a two-man team. Two men were issued their knives and compasses again, but this time they were also given a 20-foot rope. You see this assignment was to scale a mountain, free hand, using just the rope, get to the top, tie the rope around each others waist so that there was three or four feet separating them, and wait. Wait for what you may ask. They stand there until a helicopter that is dragging a rope with a hook on the end, flies by and hooks the rope tied to the men. The men would then slam together, be lifted, and brought safely to the ground. Are these guys tough or what?

Competition between these soldiers was fierce. They were the best of the best and they wanted to prove it. The rifle range was a good place for that. All 20 Special Forces trainees were poised to show their prowess. They were shooting assault sniper rifles at 200 yards to start and there wasn't one shot that stayed from the bulleye. At 500 yards, 10 soldiers scored 4 out of 5 center shots and 10 were a perfect 5 of 5. Peter was one of them. At 1,000 yards, 3 soldiers had a miss, but were still 4 out of 5. Magnificent shooting, but not good enough. Only Peter Conti and Lee Roy Sikes, a country boy from Birmingham Alabama, were left. They were shooting at 1,500 yards, almost a mile from the target. Two rounds would determine the winner of this competition. This wasn't training anymore all now; this was a sporting event. Lee Roy had the first shot and didn't waste it.

"Bulleye," the spotter shouted out as he pulled his head back from the fixed binoculars.

"Nice shooting Lee Roy," said Peter.

"Thanks man, have at it."

Peter took careful aim. He adjusted the tripod. The rifles they were shooting were equipped with powerful scopes, but the wind was a big factor, plus the amount that the projectile would drop over the distance traveled. Peter took all that into consideration and squeezed the trigger.

"Bull's eye," the spotter yelled again.

Lee Roy set up for his final shot and squeezed the trigger.

"Miss," shouted the spotter.

Peter took his final shot and didn't miss. Two bull's eyes from almost a mile away, that's not good shooting. That's incredible. Peter gained the respect of his peers, and acclaim by his superiors, that day.

Training continued. They were taught to survive on nothing and gain weight while they were doing it. They could see in the dark better than an owl. They could hold their breath underwater for an extraordinary length of time. They could walk into a room, turn off the light switch, and kill a man before the lights went out. These were dangerous men. The best our country could offer. When training was over, Peter and his cohort's mission had been accomplished; these soldiers joined an elite group, a group respected and feared by all. Wherever they went people would stare. These were special soldiers. They were flat out killing machines that wore the badge of courage, strength, and honor on their heads as a symbol to all. They are SPECIAL FORCES GREEN BERET.

Vietnam

(A Hero Emerges)

"DaNang, what a shit hole, thought Peter as he stepped off the transport that brought him here from Fort Bragg.

"Hey man, fill me in about this hole," Peter asked his high school friend Jim Asmith, who he just happened to bump into on his way to his quarters. Jim had been stationed in DaNang for almost three months.

"Oh, it's really nice. If you stray to far from the camp at night alone you have a very good chance of being killed, for a starter. We're hated here. The locals all wish we would die. The food stinks, the hookers are diseased, and the beer is almost always warm. You've got to know someone to get ice. I know someone by the way. Every time you go out on an op you figure it's your last. The hours are long, the pay stinks, and you have a perpetual case of athlete's foot. The weather is ridiculous, and it's almost impossible to sleep. Other than that, it's fine."

"Jesus Christ," Peter uttered.

"I don't think he visits here," was Jim's response.

"How long have you been here?"

"Eighty-one days, but who's counting." "The truth is when you're here the days don't matter till, you're a short timer with twenty-one days left, then days matter. You got orders yet? I'm sure that you're not staying here with us peons."

"I'll find out in the morning. And I don't plan on peeing on anyone."

"Well, buddy, it's good to see ya. Welcome to Vietnam."

Peter reported to the Captain exactly at 0800, as ordered.

"Do you have my new orders, Sir?"

"Yes, Sergeant right here." He pulled an envelope from his drawer and read them before he handed them to Peter. "You are to report to Po Jing, by August 1, connect with 4 other Green Berets led by a Captain Olsen and await further orders from a Major Eller. That's all that it says."

"How do I to get there, Sir?"

"I have supply trucks heading there tomorrow. You can catch a ride with them. Report to Sergeant Meyers at the motor pool in the morning 0700. He'll direct you to the caravan."

"Thank you, Sir"

"Good luck Sergeant. Dismissed."

Peter caught up with Sergeant Nicholas Meyers early the next morning. Meyers was a cantankerous, weathered soldier who'd been around the block a few times. This wasn't this man's first dance. Meyers told Peter he was informed that he'd have a passenger and that they would ride together. They would be in the lead truck.

Four trucks loaded with supplies going to Po Jing took off right on time. Their orders were to drop their load there, fill up with their needed supplies and head back to camp that same day. Each truck had a driver and a soldier who rode shotgun. It was only about a two-hour trip, but as always, when traveling in the jungles of Vietnam, hazard was involved.

"Green Beret huh. You guys are some bad ass sons of bitches," said Sergeant Meyers, like that was just a given.

"That's what they say."

"We've been told you guys can jump into an enemy foxhole with just a knife, kill everything that moves in there and come out without breaking a sweat."

"I heard that too."

"You don't talk much, Conti."

"You know Sarge, I 'm just busy keeping my eyes peeled." "There are gook here in Nam you know."

"Yeah, I heard that myself."

After awhile they came to a narrow spot in the road, not that it was much of a road. The oversized trail was not only narrower; the jungle was thicker here too. So, Meyers slowed down a bit.

"Now's a good time to peel back those eyes. We've lost a truck or two in this area before."

Not a minute after he said that, a bullet entered the windshield and caught Meyers in the shoulder. Peter grabbed the steering wheel with his left hand and turned the truck, angling it between two trees. He shut it down and pulled Sergeant Meyers out and laid him next to the truck. The back trucks followed. As all the men huddled together at Sergeant Meyers' side, Peter spoke.

"Anybody see where that shot came from?"

"I think I saw a puff of smoke from the top of that crest, Sergeant," answered Private Johnson.

Three more shells hit the lead truck as they spoke.

"I see it. Just left of that clump of trees on the right. Anybody else see that?"

"Yes, Sergeant. Came the response from a number of the men."

"Johnson, see to the Sergeant's wounds. I'm sure there's a first aid kit in every one of these vehicles and sit tight till I get back. I'm in command now that Sergeant Meyers is out of commission. I'm going to do recon on our position and try to find out our situation."

He continued with," Take up positions guarding the trucks and supplies. Private Rogers, grab the set of walkie-talkies I saw under the front seat here. Keep listening for my orders. Do not try and contact me. If you don't hear from me, or I'm not back in two hours, turn around and get back to camp. Is that clear?"

"Yes Sergeant," was said simultaneously.

Peter, armed with a M-14, a knife, and a couple of grenades, took off. Seconds later he was out of sight. Moving like a cat he headed to where those shots were fired.

When he was approximately five hundred yards from the suspected area, he saw movement in some bushes just in front of him. He settled in, becoming almost invisible with his surroundings. Two Cong were sneaking their way towards the trucks. They had the misfortune of passing directly past Peter's location. Peter let the first one go by. As the second one passed, Peter grabbed him, covered his mouth with his hand and plunged a knife directly into his back. Peter ripped the knife upwards piercing his heart. Immediate death. The slight commotion made the lead man turn, to investigate. He got a thrown knife, the knife Peter just pulled out of the other guys back, stuck in his forehead for his trouble. Peter had dispatched these two without a single sound. He then pulled his knife out of the second man's head, wiped it, and hunkered down, well hidden, to listen for more of their friends. After five minutes of silence Peter headed again for that clump of trees. It wasn't but another 100 yards and Peter ran into another unfortunate foe. He broke the man's neck before he even saw Peter. Fifty yards further up he crossed a small ravine that just screamed out trap. He skirted the small indentation and circled back. Sitting in wait were three more soldiers, eyes peeled on the ravine crossing. They heard a shot and there was only two. They started to scramble but before they could dive into any hiding spot, there was one. Peter slithered towards the remaining gook, his heart pounding. Moments later he heard a slight rustling of a bush to his left and Peter's M-14 spit out a volley of three rounds. Peter moved a few yards from were he fired so his enemy couldn't pinpoint his exact location and waited. He had no idea if he had dispatched the third man. After what seemed an hour but, was probably only minutes Peter silently meandered to a spot where he could view the area behind the bush he fired into. There laid number three, dead as a doornail. As he was surveying his surroundings, he heard two more shots coming from the spot he was advancing to. They were still firing on the convoy. The shots sounded like they were coming from high up. Peter figured, sniper. Probably perched in a tree. Oftentime's snipers have spotters, guys who do the targeting for them. Peter searched the trees for both possibilities, when suddenly another shot was fired, badly timed for that sniper. Peter located the shooter and within seconds he had the spotter too. Pop, ten seconds later, pop again, two quick shots from Peter's M-14. Two Viet Cong dropped like acorns falling from a tree. Peter searched the area for more enemy soldiers. None found. He called in.

"All clear, 8 enemy soldiers down."

"Yes, Sergeant, good work Sergeant. What are your orders now Sergeant?"

"First, how is Sergeant Meyers?"

"Complaining, Sergeant. Wants to know where you went, Sergeant."

"Sounds like he is as tough as he looks. Sit tight, I'm on my way back. I want to check our backside before we take off."

"Yes Sergeant."

Peter circled back. It wasn't over yet. Four more enemy soldiers were approaching the trucks following the road behind them. The key word here is WERE. Peter intercepted the rear attack before it started. He strangled one, knifed one and shot the other two. He left the bodies where they lay and headed back to the trucks.

Peter took a moment to gather his thoughts. He just killed twelve men like he was squirrel hunting on a Sunday morning. He's been on Vietnam soil less than 72 hours and he's already taken lives. His head was spinning but he surveyed his situation and it only took a few moments for reality to set in. What he did was save lives, nine of them. This is war. More words of advice from his father struck home, "If you have to kill someone you kill em. It's war." That being said, Peter still walked to the road with a heavy heart.

Peter got back to the trucks. He informed the men of the happening, like it was nothing special, and helped get the Sergeant back in the truck. Of course, this time Peter was doing the driving.

The other men got back into their trucks. Knowing that what they had just witnessed, no matter what Sergeant Peter Conti Green Beret, called it, it was something special. More than special, it was flat out heroic.

"What the hell happened out there?" asked Meyers.

"I went to see who was doing all the shooting. It kind of pissed me off that one of their bullets went awry and hit a friend of mine. When I was walking out there, two gooks came running out of the jungle, tripped and fell on my knife. I danced with another, but he was dead tired. Three more decided they didn't want to breath anymore, so I obliged them. I shot at the other two, who were up in trees. I probably missed em but luckily, they fell out of the trees and killed themselves. Then on my way back, I stumbled into four of their buddies who must have been lost. Why else would they be headed to our trucks? They won't be finding their way back at all. I'll tell ya Sarge, it ain't safe out here."

Meyers had a painful laugh and stuck out his hand, "Thank you soldier you're something else. I've always know'd it but now I'm sure. Green Berets are some bad mother fuckers."

Moments later, Peter gave the Sergeant a full and actual report, which was required, since Meyers was the man in charge. Meyers took mental notes knowing he would have to report all this to the Captain when they returned. What Meyers didn't say was he wanted to make sure of the facts so that Peter Conti got the credit he deserved. People get medals for what he'd just done.

Peter's Green Beret Team
(The Five-Man Stealth Unit)
(The Meet Up)

"Sergeant Burk? Captain Olsen said I should bunk here with you. My name is Conti, Peter Conti."

"Welcome Conti, Peter Conti. Name's Nigel but my friends call me Nitro." "Throw your stuff down and make yourself at home."

"Thanks Sergeant. Does that name Nitro, have anything to do with explosives?" Peter asked sarcastically.

"It has everything to do with explosives. There ain't a thing that's ever been built that I can't blow up."

"You don't have anything in here that can go boom, do you?"

"Nah, they frown on that here," he laughed. "How long have you been over?"

"I'm green."

"Well, if you're the hotshot Green Beret that just made the grand entrance into camp, it doesn't sound like you're too green."

"Jesus, man. How fast does word travel in this camp?"

Nitro responded with, "You can't take a shit without everybody knowing. Hell, what else is there to do? Besides everybody likes to hear when Charlie takes it in the ass. Nice going, Conti! Every time a fellow Green Beret comes up smelling like a rose, it just builds on our mystique. GI's think we're Gods. I love it. Welcome."

"Thanks, Sarge."

"Call me Nitro. What did happen out there this morning, man?"

They talked for a short while. Burk had to go check on something he was cooking up. He has to work on the outskirts of the camp, for obvious reasons. Peter got organized and got as comfortable as he was going to get. He was anxious to meet the other guys but more anxious to know what their orders were, and where he was going to fit in. He started jotting down a note to Jackie but decided what happened in Nam was going to stay in Nam. She and his entire family are worried enough.

At 1700 hours, Captain Orin Olsen stood at the flap at the entrance to the two Sergeants tent.

"Chow," he shouted.

Peter stepped out and, of course, recognized that standing next to the Captain were two more Green Berets.

"Burk with you?" asked the Captain.

"No Sir," said Peter as he saluted the Captain and the other officer standing next to him. "Said he'd catch up with us at the mess tent."

"Peter Conti, this is Lieutenant Joseph La Vaca and Sergeant Tom Tully, the rest of our interesting group."

"Lieutenant, Sergeant, good to meet you."

"Po Jing Pete is the nickname the entire camp is already calling you Peter. WOW. HE'S REAL. Sorry, couldn't resist that Conti, but man you stood this camp on its ear. Hell, by the time the boys are done passing this story around, you will have killed an entire platoon single handedly," said Sergeant Tully with a big smile on his face. "Good job Sergeant. It's good to have a man like you on our team."

Sergeant Thomas J. Tully enlisted in the army in 64 became a Green Beret in 65 and is serving his second tour in Nam. All Green Berets are more than efficient when it comes to weaponry, but some are what you would call, let's say specialist on one weapon in particular. Tom is Vietnam's answer to William Tell. What an archer. Put a bow in this man's hands and he could hit a dime tossed in the air from 100 paces. He could do the apple thing, but he hasn't found a volunteer that would put the apple on their head. It wouldn't take a genius to figure out the handle Tully was labeled with. Everybody just calls him "Tell."

"Italian?" asked the Lieutenant.

"Yes Sir. Full blooded."

"Paisan. Welcome aboard. Gotta ask, if you just got to Nam, you probably just had shore leave, I would seriously appreciate it, if you wouldn't mind telling me, what your mother made for dinner the night before you shipped out?"

"No problem Lieutenant. On my last night before shipping out, we had veal cutlets, sliced thin and breaded with fresh lemon. I don't know what your family calls fried eggplant, but we call it mulenjohnny, a side of penne, salad, and fresh bread."

"Stop it, you're killing me, you bastard. Why did I ask?"

Lieutenant Joseph Anthony La Vaca. ROTC, University of Pennsylvania, class of 68. Went directly into Special Forces training and shipped into Vietnam as a Green Beret six months ago. They say he can walk across a stick of butter and not leave a footprint. He moves like a cat and can be as invisible as a ghost, a good man to have on your team.

They shared a meal consisting of some form of meat, no one knew exactly what kind of meat but meat all the same with canned potatoes and green beans. La Vaca complained the entire meal. They all wondered what their orders would be, but no one speculated. The Captain said he really had no idea but that when he found out, they would find out. When that was, he didn't know, but he expected Major Eller to show up with their orders any day. Waiting is always hard but waiting in camp when the fighting is all around you is a whole lot better than anywhere in the jungle.

"Sarge, I mean Nitro, what's the story with the Captain? He didn't say much at chow," Peter asked as the men entered their tent.

"Good man and a fine officer," came the reply.

"Yeah, I could guess that, but what's his story?

"He's at the end of his tour. That I know. The word is that, if you were going to rob a bank, he'd be the guy you'd want to draw up the plan. He's a braineac. Is that a word?"

"I don't know but I get your gist."

37

"Well, I think I understand this little group. According to what you've told me about the Lieutenant and Tell, we have a team made up of Robin Hood, a ghost, a brain, and the mad bomber. That kind of sounds like a pretty formidable team. I'm still trying to figure out where I fit in."

"Oh, the Captain checked your shit out as soon as he knew you were joining this team. He said you're our marksman."

"We can all shoot man. I don't get it," replied Peter.

"Yeah, we can all shoot, but the word that came down from HQ is you could shoot the dick off a hummingbird from a mile away. If I had to make a guess here Pete, I'd say, sniper.

The Medals
(Peter Becomes the Most Decorated Soldier Out of the State of New York)
(He and His Team Were Killing Machines)

These five men were instrumental in the success of numerous campaigns. Saving American soldiers lives and accomplishing tasks that only men with their skills could even attempt. They were a stealth unit that had the respect of everyone who knew of there existence. These guys were trained killers. They killed anyone who would get in the way of them accomplishing their mission. Simply stated, they were bigtime heroes.

After all their heroics in Vietnam a special day came. The day Captain Orin Olsen and Sergeant Peter Conti would receive medals they earned while serving their country.   La Vaca, Tell and Nitro received their medals in over there, where they were still fighting. The Conti's and Jackie, along with Betty and the Olsens (Orin's wife and his parents), sat in the grandstands in readiness waiting for Peter and Orin to receive their commendations. They were talking and laughing and had already accepted each other as one big happy family. It would be impossible to explain the pride they all felt. They had no idea what their sons were being honored for because neither of the men liked to talk about things that went on over there, but just the fact that they were being honored was enough.

The time came for the awards. Colonel Jorgenson, the base commander, stood in front of the two soon to be decorated soldiers and read,

"For their courage under fire, above and beyond the call of duty while engaging the enemy and executing to completion the total and utter destruction of the Tong River Bridge and the troop transport on that bridge, ultimately saving countless American soldiers lives the United States of America is proud to award, Special Forces' Green Beret Captain Orin Olsen and Special Forces' Green Beret Sergeant Peter Conti, the Bronze Star for Heroic and Meritorious Achievement,."

He pinned them on the men's chest and saluted. They returned his salute and he took three steps back and read again.

"The Purple Heart for Military Merit is awarded to Special Forces' Green Beret Sergeant Peter Conti for injuries obtained while engaging the enemy during the execution of his duties at the Tong River Bridge."

He pinned it on Peter's chest and saluted. Peter returned his salute and the Colonel took three steps back and read again

"For their courage under fire, above and beyond the call of duty, while engaged in the elimination of the defenses protecting Fong Lo Peak, which lead to a complete victory in the Capturing of Fong Lo Peak, again saving the lives of countless American soldiers, the United States of America is proud to award Special Forces' Green Beret Captain Orin Olsen and Special Forces' Green Beret Sergeant Peter Conti, the Silver Star, for Gallantry in Action."

Again, he pinned the medals on the men's chests and saluted Again they returned his salute. He took three steps back and read again,

"For courage under fire, above and beyond the call of duty, while transporting supplies from the base camp at DaNang to the base camp at Po Jing, in order to defend and protect the lives of his men, he single handedly, without regard to his own safety and life, eliminated an entire patrol of enemy soldiers, the United States of America is proud to award Special Forces' Green Beret Sergeant Peter Conti, the Distinguished Service Cross, For Valor, "

He pinned the second highest award the country gives, second only to the Congressional Medal of Honor, on Peter's chest and saluted, Peter returned his salute one more time.

The Colonel stepped back and saluted both men, congratulated them, and dismissed them. When they started to walk away, the people and soldiers in attendance cheered like they were at a football game and their team just scored. It was a proud moment for both men.

Thomas Conti stood and as he applauded a tear of complete and utter pride slid down his face. As he sat there and listened to the pure acts of bravery, the undeniable courage, the selflessness, all he could think of was, his son down there getting those medals. That was his son that had earned the respect and admiration of his peers. That was his son who was simply stated, a HERO.

The rest of that day and the next were days of celebration. There were pictures and interviews strictly for Army propaganda and a couple of just fun parties for the men and their families, but it finally came to an end. It was time to go. The Olsen and Conti families checked out of the hotel and after all the hugging and hand shaking both families headed to their cars. Peter was going home. Home for good. The Contis loaded everything in the trunk and just before they pulled out Peter excused himself. He had to say goodbye to someone first.

"Captain."

"It's Orin now Pete."

"Not to me." "I simply have no words."

"None needed. You know sometimes men are just meant to be in the same place at the same time. It's called destiny. That's what happened to us 5. Couldn't explain it if we tried. I know I don't need to say this but I'm going to anyway. If you ever need me, no matter what it is, no matter when, I'll be there."

"You're right you didn't have to say it. Just like I know I don't need to say that goes the same here. A man is lucky if in his lifetime he has a friend like you. I hit the jackpot, I got 4 all at once."

"We all did," said Orin.

As Peter turned to walk away, he said, "Good luck Cap." Peter hesitated a moment and then said, "Orin, thanks for everything and I mean everything. This is not goodbye; I promise you we'll always be in touch."

"See ya buddy. And if you think of it, maybe you could invite us guys to your wedding," added Orin.

"Fuck you, that's for friends only."

They shook hands and then hugged. Peter Conti, Special Forces Green Beret, after the military ending wounds he received while blowing up the Tong River Bridge, was going home. He had to get a job.

Hero Comes Home
     (Job, Wedding Plans, Vito Bansano)

Peter came home to a hero's welcome. Jackie was overjoyed. The man she loved more than life itself was alive and home and they were getting married. Peter felt the same. All that was holding them back was he needed a job. A newspaper article beaming about Peter's heroism got the attention of all that read it. With fame came opportunity and that article led Peter to a very nice job. Peter's new boss invited Peter and Jackie to a celebratory dinner. As they ate, a surprise arose.

"Oh my God. Hello Sir," said a surprised Peter. "It's been a long time."

"Hello **my young friend**. It certainly has. I hope I'm not interrupting, I just wanted to say hello."

"I'm glad you did Sir. Let me introduce you. Vito Bansano, this is my fiancée Jacqueline Millen and my boss Paul Williams."

Vito Bansano signaled the extremely burly men who accompanied him to step back with just a flick of his hand and they immediately did. He took Jackie's hand in his, kissed it, and said,

"It's a pleasure to meet you my dear. And you Sir. Peter, I really stopped by because I wanted to tell you how proud I am of you. You made my year, kid. I even saved the damn paper. Excuse me miss, I mean I saved that wonderful newspaper article for crying out loud. Impressive, my young friend, impressive. I had to tell you that."

"Thank you, Sir. I appreciate it."

"I have to go now. It was nice meeting you both and enjoy your meal. Peter, I've taken care of your bill. Everything is on me. No need to say thanks, it's my pleasure."

Peter stood, shook his hand and quietly said, "thank you Sir." Mr. Bansano nodded and left with his entourage.

As soon as they were out of sight, Paul asked, "Peter, is that THE Vito Bansano?"

Jackie looked straight into Peter's eyes awaiting an answer. Peter, acting like it wasn't a big deal and not like he was talking about the head of the mafia, simply said. "Yes"

Peter's Dad Almost Dies
(Vito Bansano to the Rescue)

Tom Conti was dying. The blood flow to his heart wasn't sufficient to keep him alive. He needed a surgical process that only a very few doctors could perform at the time and none were available. It would take a miracle for Peter's dad to live. But miracles do happen, and one happened here when out of the blue the best surgeon in the field showed up and performed the operation. Peter's dad lived.

Peter was in tears when he thanked the doctor for saving his father's life.

"Well Peter, to be honest with you, I got a call from a friend and he asked me if I could do him a personal favor. I told him that wouldn't be a problem. So here I am. He also wanted me to tell you something."

He said to say to you, "You're welcome….**MY YOUNG FRIEND**."

Peter, with Jackie pleading with him not to go, was absolutely compelled to meet with Vito Bansano and thank him. He knew owing someone in his position a favor could be his undoing but, in this case, he didn't care. His father was alive.

"Hello, my young friend," said Vito as he stepped out of his office that's in the back of his restaurant, the Delaware Grill, and sat at his personal table. "Sit down Peter. What can I do for you?"

"Sir, I don't know how you knew about my father, but I can never thank you enough for what you've done for my family and me today. It was the nicest, most generous thing anyone has ever done for me and I rushed over to personally thank you from the bottom of my heart!" Peter had a lump in his throat when he continued full well knowing what he was about to say next could change his life forever.

"Sir, if there is anything I can do for you, Anything, please just say the word."

"First, how is your father? Second, I have eyes and ears all over the city. That's my job."

"Thanks to you Sir, my father is alive and well."

"That's great news. I'm happy for you. Understand this Peter, I told you many years ago that you made a good friend. I meant that. All I want from you is for you to be happy. This has nothing to do with my business, nothing. All I ever wanted from you you've already given me, your friendship. Not because of my position in life but because of the beautiful conversations we had and the respect you have always shown me, as a man, not because of my job. That has always meant a lot to me. You owe me nothing. Absolutely nothing. I did what friends do. That's all I did. Now get out of here and go be with your family.

Peter got up to leave and said, "God bless you sir."

The response, "Call me Vito!"

The Wedding

Jackie looked like a goddess in her flowing white wedding gown. To say she looked beautiful would not do her justice. She was exquisite. The smile on her father Mike's face as he walked her down the isle spoke volumes. The man could not be happier for his daughter. But nothing could compare to the smile Peter had, it was so big his face was starting to hurt. As she approached the altar, you could feel the culmination of two peoples' dreams coming to fruition. When their eyes met and their hands touched as far as they were concerned, they were married that second. The rest of the ceremony was just formality. Russell, Peter's best man, much to the chagrin of Sonny, Ray, and Al, beamed with pride as he handed his brother the ring, he was about to place on the ever-awaiting finger of Jackie's left hand. The three friends were groomsmen and Peter loved them all like brothers, but Russell, was his brother. Same thing with the maid of honor, Jill, Jackie's sister who held that honor. The two ushers Orin and Nigel (Nitro) looked like the war heroes they are in their dress uniforms, complete with medals. Peter's mom and dad felt such a sense of pride to be escorted to their seats by the obvious friends and comrades of their son. The two men were honored to do so. If there is such a thing as a perfect wedding, it just happened.

Just before the bride and groom took the walk back down the isle to the cheers of all who attended, a solo figure of a man who entered late and was leaving early got up to go.
Vito Bansano told Peter when Peter personally handed him the wedding invitation that although he really wanted to attend, he respectfully refused. He just didn't want his presence and reputation to be a topic of conversation at all. Not on this special occasion. He just couldn't resist attending. You see, even a man of his stature, a feared man, seldomly has friends, but when he does, enough said.

The food, the drink, the entire reception went off as planned. Wonderful. The only down-side of the whole thing was that Tom Conti could not drink. He wanted to, but doctor's orders. He still had a sip of champagne when his son Russell proposed the toast. Tom said to Theresa, "If I die, I die!"

What a fun wedding!!!!!

The Russian Mob

(A War Is Brewing)

There are two factions of organized crime in America. The Italian Mafia is the main one and has been in charge for a very long time. But in recent years, the Russian mob has been trying to move in on the action. A small war has been brewing for some time in the northeast, and Vito Bansano isn't very happy about it. Ivan Terski heads up a small army of Russians who have already stepped on a number of Bansano's deals and the Godfather isn't going to let that happen again. Boris Meco is Terski's right hand man and Milas "the Butcher" Vukavich is Meco's main man in Buffalo. These men and their rag tag crew of undesirables are making life more complicated than Vito wants.

Vito has it with Terski and the Russians. They have been interfering in his business for years and he's through with their shit. He decided to shoo him out of town buy stepping on the biggest arms deal that Terski ever put together. It was huge.

Vito was adamant when he said to Tony Sotto, his right-hand man and under boss, "I want the guns and if I know Terski, his buyers are gonna be there too. Grab the guns and the fucking money. I want it all and I especially want Terski to know I've had it with his shit. This is my town; tell him to get the fuck out. Bring a big crew. Terski's no fool. If anything goes wrong, kill them all. Understand?"

"Yes Sir. I got it. You know, this is going to start a fucking war," said Tony.

"Don't tell me what to fucking do!" he screamed. "Just do what I tell you. Now get outta here." "If they want a war, they'll get a fucking war and when it's done, they'll be done! Finito."

And so, the war started. It was going to be a blood bath.

Terski was out of his mind with hatred as he addressed a group of his guys.

"Anybody recognizes any of those assholes. I know they were Bansano's guys. Who else could it be? You guys know any of those motherfuckers?"

"I know who one of them was for sure boss," answered Boris Meco. "The big guy with the tatoo of a barbell on his hand was Tiny Gatta, definitely one of Bansano's men."

"Gatta, Tiny Gatta, I want that motherfucker dead," screamed Terski, with spit flying from his mouth as he yelled every word. Dead!! If those mother fuckin dagos want a war, they got one.

"Vukavich, I want that fucking Gatta dead," ordered Terski.

The Pregnancy
(It Took 6 Years but Finally)
and

The Tragedy

It was a beautiful morning. Sun shinning, birds singing, and Peter was whistling a happy tune when his lovely wife came out of the house to hop in the car. They were heading to her obstetricians for a routine checkup. Finally, after six long years of trying, she was pregnant. They couldn't be happier.

Jackie opened the car door to a very nice surprise; Peter had a beautiful bouquet of **a dozen long stem white roses** perched on her seat waiting for her.

"Peter, you never cease to amaze me. You know how much I love **white roses**. They are the happiest flowers in the world."

"Jackie, in case you didn't know, **you ARE MY white rose**."

"I love you Peter!"

"Thanks."

"Thanks, God you're so romantic."

"Let me rephrase that. Jackie, I love you more every single day. So much that I can't wait until tomorrow. I love you sweetheart."

Without saying a word, she leaned in and kissed Peter like she did when he just returned from the war.

"Thank you darling, thank you so much. You are so thoughtful. I think you just might be the best husband in the entire world."

"Aww shucks mam, it weren't nothing," he said in a southern accent.

"Yes, it was BUT you know what would top off this wonderful morning? A Dutch Crunch bagel. I have got this overwhelming urge for one."

"A Dutch Crunch bagel, aye, aye Mam, anything for you, you pain in the ass." Peter replied knowing full well he had absolutely no choice in the matter. He knew that wasn't a request…it was an order. They had to pass the Bagels R Us on Niagara Falls Blvd. right on the way anyway. So off they went.

Entering the bagel shop, Peter noticed a semi familiar face sitting at the first table beside the door. It was one of the guys he'd seen a number of times at the Delaware Grill. He didn't know his name. The guy recognized Peter as well and nodded as he and his wife walked in. Peter gave a polite nod back and then reached for Jackie's hand. They ordered the Dutch Crunch bagel Jackie was craving and Peter ordered a cinnamon roll. They grabbed their order and sat in the back of the store, far from the gentleman Peter knew as one of Vito's men.

Tony Gatta, the Russian's target, was known to his partners in crime as Tiny because of his size. He was as big as a house. He stopped every morning at 10:00 AM like clockwork at the Bagel's R Us for a sesame bagel and 2 strong cups of black coffee. This day was no different.

After enjoying her bagel, Jackie looked at her watch and said, "Honey, we have to leave shortly, or we'll be late. But first I have to go to the ladies' room, OK. So why don't you finish up your coffee and we'll go when you're done."

"Yes, dear," he replied as he slugged down his hot drink.

She came back and he grabbed her hand and they walked to the front door. Gatta stood up just as they got there. He was leaving too and as they approached, he politely opened the door for them. Jackie stepped through the door and as she did, she turned to Peter.

"Sweetheart, I left my sweater on the chair. Would you get it for me please?"

"Sure Jackie."

Jackie walked out the door and Gatta followed. As Peter pulled his wife's sweater from the back of the chair, he heard a sound he would never forget for the rest of his life.

BANG BANG BANG BANG BANG BANG BANG BANG BANG BANG.

Peter rushed past the now squatting patrons in the shop who were ducking from the flying glass coming from the front window and the glass door. He stepped over a young couple that was obviously hit from the borage of bullets coming from the machine gun fire. He

49

jumped over the mutilated body of Tiny Gatta and slid to his knees beside the still body of his bleeding wife. She was hit twice, once in the shoulder and once in the chest. Peter's life flashed before his eyes. He did all he could to stop the bleeding all the while pleading to his unconscious wife. "Please don't leave me! Please don't leave me." "I love you Jackie, I love you."

Jackie was gone and as far as Peter was concerned, so was his life.

Grief Turns to Hatred

Peter sat on a chair in his living room stareing at the television. The thing is the television wasn't turned on. He was so lost he didn't know what to do next. His grief was so deep he could feel pain in his heart, and it wasn't medical. A piece of it was missing. He turned the TV on just to end the dead silence. The Channel 2 News was on and reporting:

"This morning in Kenmore, a suburb just outside of the city limits of Buffalo, a person or persons unknown, but alleged to be part of a Russian crime syndicate, perpetrated an execution style assassination. The suspicion that the Russian syndicate is somehow involved in this despicable act is predicated on the fact that the assumed victim, 43-year-old Anthony J. Gatta is allegedly part of another crime syndicate commonly known as the Italian Mafia. The drive by shooting occurred at 10:24 AM just as Gatta was exiting the building. Three bystanders were fatally wounded as machine gun bullets riddled the entire entranceway of the building just behind me. The Bagels R US is located on the corner of Niagara Falls Blvd. and Delaware Ave. The names and identities of the other victims are being withheld until their families can be notified. More details should be upcoming, and we will keep you informed every step of the way. Buffalo police fear we may have a mob war on our hands, and they intend to nip this in the bud before it gets out of hand. Tell that to the families of the three innocent bystanders who lost their lives this morning."

This is Mary Motta, reporting live from the Bagels R US in Kenmore.

Peter's expression turned from grief to hatred. The killing machine persona he left in Vietnam started building back up inside Peter until it hit a crescendo. Thoughts of his life lashed through his head. A new Peter arose. The Russian scum that just took Jackie's life were about to face an enemy that would be their worst nightmare. A cold-hearted killing machine with nothing but revenge on his mind. A man that was more dangerous than any man they have ever faced before and for one simple reason. This man had no fear because he didn't care if he lived or died. This enemy would and is going to hunt them down like dogs until he or the last one of them is dead.

Peter stood up, the blood rushing to his face from shear adrenalin, stared into the television set and screamed at the top of his lungs.

"I" LL KILL THEM ALL, EVERY SINGLE FUCKING ONE. I" LL KILL THEM ALL.

Revenge
(Vito was Collateral Damage)

>Peter started killing and Milas Vukavich was the first to feel his wrath. Peter left **a single white rose** next to every victim's body, a gesture meaningless to all, except Peter Conti.

>Knowing Vito would be blamed for the killings, Peter confronted Vito and his men and confessed that he was the guy the news media were now calling THE FLOWER MAN.

"Vito, I have to say this, and I'll lay it out straight. I know you're in the middle of what they're calling a gang war. I didn't start it. It started when those fucking Russians put a hit on Tony Gatta. This you all know. What you may not know is those two-bit Russian punks killed my wife at the same time. She was standing next to Gatta when it happened. You understand what I'm saying. **They killed my wife.**"

Revenge, revenge is the most powerful motivation a man can have. Make no mistake, I have it running through my veins. You guys are thinking retaliate but I'm thinking revenge. Vito is right. I know how to kill. I'm good at it. Real good. You think you're bad. I could kill three of you with a dull spoon before you could blink an eye. I say this not in a threatening way at all. Vito's not my enemy he's my friend. He's more than a friend to me. I'm telling you this cause its just a fact. I'm telling you this, so you know I'm not spinning some kind of bullshit yarn. Those motherfuckers killed my wife. They will all pay with their lives, I swear it; so, Vito, it's up to you. Either kill me now for what I've done or let me go and I'll kill more of those sons of bitches."

"Jesus Christ Conti. Jesus Christ. You know what you've got yourself in the middle of my young friend?" Said the saddened mafia boss after hearing all this.

"Yes, I do Vito."

Vito turned to his men and said, "Our every move has been watched by every cop in the city. This is good what he said." He turned to Peter and said, "I hate to say this, but Peter you have my blessings."

That moment triggered a turn of events that put unforeseen wheels into motion. Peter was on a rampage. His killing persona was in full bloom and the Russians blamed Vito Bansano. Terski had to do something big and he did.

They found Vito Bansano laying next to his car in the parking lot of the Delaware Grill with two bullets lodged in the back of his head. Terski got his revenge.

Peter watched his television, with even more hate in his eyes than before, as the news of Vito's murder was being reported,

"What the police are calling a war between the crime syndicates hit a new high, minutes ago, when the body of Italian Crime Boss Vito Bansano was found shot to death on his establishment's parking lot. Bansano, known to the police as THE GODFATHER, was 73 years old, unmarried, with no children. Bansano owned and operated the Delaware Grill located on the 24th block of Delaware Ave. On the outside it is a quaint looking Italian eatery, but police have always thought of the restaurant as a front for many criminal activities. The police now feel that a blood bath could erupt from this latest ruthless killing and all officers are on watch. This is a dangerous time to be living in this city. Please stay close to your homes."

Peter raced to the Delaware Grill and confronted Vito's men.

Cops were milling around the restaurant like ants. News people filled the street and police were directing crowds away from the area. Tony Sotto saw Peter and yelled to the police,

"Officer, let that guy in. He's related to Mr. Bansano."

Peter walked into a frenzy of hot-tempered, livid Italians ready to load up and finish this war. No one, counting the cops was going to stop them from putting Terski in a grave. No one that is, until Peter walked in. He surveyed the confusion and listened before he said,

"Stop Goddamn it. Think for a Goddamn minute."

Sotto retorted with, "Your flower man bullshit aint gonna work this time Conti."

"This isn't about the fucking flower man, Goddamn it Tony. This isn't about killing Terski either. This is about Vito. All about Vito. I understand. You want to go out and kill those fucking Russian pricks right fucking now. I got news for you, running around half-cocked and stupidly killing a few of these sons of a bitchen Russians is exactly what Terski wants. Yeah, he might lose a few men, but, in the end, the cops take you out and he gets it all. Use your fucking heads."

Frankie Andolino shouted at Peter, "Who the fuck do you think you are Conti telling us what to do?"

"SHUT THE FUCK UP FRANKIE!" screamed Peter at the top of his lungs. He continued with, "You want the Russians. I want them too, even more, mark my words. They will die. We're going kill them all. I got a way. I got a fuckin way of killing EVERY FUCKING ONE... ALL AT ONCE!!!! And we won't have to fire a shot.

The room got very quiet very fast.

We Will Kill Them All
(One Fell Swoop)

"Sure, you mind telling us Conti what the hell you're talking about?" asked Nino Torisi.

"Yeah, spit it out, we're all getting pretty tired of your shit anyway," added Vittorio Sordi, thinking he was speaking for the whole group.

"First, Frankie, I planned this with Vito and needed something before you guys could be filled in. Second, **don't ever talk to me like that again, you understand me Sordi. I hope you do.** Here it is in a nutshell. I'm going to set up a meeting with the Russians, call it a truce. We share everything, I tell Terski there's enough for everybody if we don't get greedy. We eat, we drink, and we work a few things out. What they won't know is I'm going to do one more thing at this meeting. I'm going to poison them. I'm going to poison them and watch them all die. All at once."

Gino Paladino laughed out loud, and said, "That's funny. You think you're going to be able to get him to gather his men and come to a meeting with us and you think they're not going to suspect a thing. That is fucking hilarious. This is even funnier; we're going to all be together eating and drinking shit and they're the only ones that are getting poisoned. No fucking way they're falling for that. How you plan on pulling that trick off, Conti?"

"I'm not. We're going to get poisoned too."

"What the fuck Conti. You losing your fucking marbles?" injected Frankie Andolino.

"No Frankie. I still got my marbles. I also have a shitload of antidote that we'll all be taking before the meeting. They die. We don't. Done."

"Jesus Christ, where did you get the shit?" asked Frankie.

"Tony Sotto here from his black-market connection. He's already got the stuff. It's done. All I got to do is set up the meeting. That's the hard part."

"The big question is, how do you plan on getting that done?" asked Sotto.

"Here's what I'm thinking. Terski don't know me from a bag of shit. If any of you tried to meet with the guy, he'd off you before you got a word out of your mouth. But me, if I contact him and portray myself as Vito's consigliere (advisor), he might just listen. I'll give him some song and dance about both sides taking a beating and losing guys left and right. I'll convince him that, if this keeps up, there won't be anybody left on either side. Everything, all the work, all the scams, all the setups, and all the money, everything we got goes up in smoke. That will get his attention. I'll follow that with this idea, we join forces, and call it a partnership. I'll then say let's face it, there's plenty for everybody. I'll propose a meeting. I'm going to suggest someplace over the bridge in Canada. No cops there, and if we set it up right, no one to bother us. It will be a business meeting out in the country somewhere. There will be no tricks, no guns, no gimmicks, and no fucking around, strictly business. I'll tell him we can work out the details together. I'll tell him it only makes sense that everyone from both sides should be there. That way we can make sure we divide up everything fair. We'll eat, we'll drink, and we'll all leave rich men. If he goes for it, they die."

He went for it.
The Meeting

The meeting went perfectly. There was some hesitation but each man (the Russians) realized fair was fair and no more competition meant more money for everybody. The Italians played their parts to the fullest. Terski and Peter argued a bit. One gave in a little than the other until both sides felt like this was going to work out great.

When the negotiating was over, they partied; they drank and ate like kings. All provided by the Russians. When the meeting was coming to a close, Peter brought out a few bottles of Vodka. He rolled it out on a table full of shot glasses and poured each glass full.

"This is the one of the finest Vodkas in the world and a fitting end to a perfect meeting. To our new partners and to the shitload of money for all," toasted Peter as he drank a shot glass full first.

Then each man grabbed a shot and raised his glass. All but one, Victor Benko.

Peter said, "Victor?"

"I don't drink."

Peter said, "I'll drink one for you my new friend," and drank another.

Terski toasted, "To the end and the beginning."

They all drank. After a minute or two, the first guy, Mikal Stavro, stumbled as he fell, Peter picked up a fork from the table and stuck it into Victor Benko's throat. Killed him on the spot. The Russians started falling like bowling pins.

As Terski went to his knees, Peter walked over to him, pushed him down on his back and said,

"All of this was for my wife," he said as he showed him a long stem white rose.

Terski's last words were, "Fuck You!"

Peter answered with, "Rot in hell you Cocksucker!"

Peter threw a long stem white rose on Terski and each of the Russian bodies, thus taking the suspicion off of Vito's men and placing it on THE FLOWER MAN.

The Italians wiped the place clean, grabbed the booze and the glasses, and headed to the door. Just before they exited, Tony Sotto stopped all the men. They all looked at Peter when Tony asked,

"WHAT'S NEXT BOSS?"

Peter thought for a second before he spoke and quickly realized he was too deep for there to be any other answer, he replied,

"WE'RE JUST GETTING STARTED!"

That's the story. That's how Peter Conti, a clean-cut all-American boy from the suburbs became,

THE GODFATHER.

That's exactly how it happened. Now he had to live with his decision. Peter Conti, The Godfather, there are no books to guide him, only instinct. He was a businessman, and he was going to run the whole thing like a business, with one exception: If need be, killing would be involved.

Peter Conti is gone. Long live The Godfather.

* End of Prologue

Chapter 2

MAFIA, LLC
The Conti Story Continues

Peter sat staring at nothing. His whole world was gone. He was able to keep his family and friends from knowing what had transpired but he knew that he couldn't keep what was happening now away from them. Quitting his job and taking over the previously owned restaurant of a Mafia boss was something that he couldn't just shrug off. His life was going to change no matter how he tried to explain it away. Everything was going to be different. He tried to move back into their house but couldn't stand staying there, just too many memories of Jackie. He put it up for sale.

Next step. Telling his family and friends. But telling them what? That's the question. He started out by talking with his three lifelong buddies.

"What the fuck are you talking about?" screamed a frantic Sony Lippa, with Ray and Al standing right beside him. "Let me get this straight. Vito Bansano, the fuckin murdered Mafia boss, left you this fuckin restaurant in his will. That's what you're telling us?"

"Yeah."

"Come on Pete. What the hell is going on?" retorted a somewhat calmer Ray Baldi.

"Fill us in brother," asked Alfonso Epolito.

"I can't. I love you guys but some stuff I just can't say."

"This is fuckin nuts!" shouted Sonny.

"Calm down Sonny. You guys know my life has changed since I lost Jackie. This is part of it."

"Part of what? Look Pete, I'll calm down when you tell us the truth. What is happening here?"

"Sonny, there are some things better left unknown. Things that if you knew could and would put you in a compromising position. This is all I can say right now, and it has to be enough. People are going to ask you a lot of questions about me. Not just people we know either. Reporters, cops, even strangers out of nowhere, all because Vito left me this restaurant. It's normal. Everyone will assume that I'm connected. Here's what you should tell anyone who's asking about me. You tell them that all you know is that Peter met Vito Bansano when he was young and still in college at Buffalo State. He used to eat at his restaurant pretty much every day. It was close to school. He didn't know who the guy was. They used to talk and soon became friends, it just happened; he was a good man to Peter, period. When he died, he left Peter the restaurant. Peter decided he didn't want to travel for a job anymore and liked the idea of being a restaurateur. That's all you have to say. It's a little more involved than that but that's all anybody needs to know."

"What do you mean a little more involved?" asked Al.

"I don't know right now. Vito left some instructions in his will that he wants me to take care of for him. He never had a family and he obviously felt close enough to me to do that. He left me some money and some other stuff too."

"This is too much Peter." "What have you got yourself into?" said Sonny disgustedly.

"Look, I owe the man. I never told anyone this but when my father had the heart attack, the doctors flat out said, unless a miracle happened, he was going to die. Vito Bansano was the miracle. He called in a favor, and the number one surgeon in the whole damn country came and saved my father's life. I went to Vito to thank him. You know what Vito told me, he said I owed him nothing. He said that's what friends do for one another. So, I'm going to return the favor and follow the instructions he left me in his will."

"Peter, the guy was the head of a Mafia family, man. The people around him are still here. This smells very suspicious. He's gone. Let it rest," added Ray.

"There are many reasons for me not to be involved but I'm already involved. The Russian scum that killed my Jackie are gone and no matter what, Vito had something to do with it. It's you guys that have to let this rest because I'm not."

"And what are we supposed to do?" asked Sonny.

"Only one thing. Vito said this to me a long time ago and now I'll say it to you. Don't come around here. This place is off limits. Our friendship will live on forever, that you can count on, but things go on here, things that would be better for you not to know. Things that you can't be around."

"This is fucking unbelievable," said Sonny shaking his head and throwing his hands in the air.

"Jesus Christ Peter," added Ray.

"What are you going to tell your family? The entire city knows the Delaware Grill is a Mafia hang out. I don't know what to say Pete," injected Al.

"Guys, I don't have any answers right now. Let me see how this whole thing plays out.
 Just trust me for now. When people ask questions about me, your answer has got to be that you know nothing. Cause you don't and it's got to stay that way. It will all work out, but for now I own the Delaware Grill and that is my new job."

"Pete, we're with you no matter what. You know that," said Sonny. "This is just mind-boggling. The Mafia Peter?"

"No Sonny, not me. 'm just a restaurant owner."

With that said, Tony Sotto, Vic Desica, and Nino Torisi, all associates Of Vito Bansano, walked into the restaurant. Sotto walked over to where the four friends were sitting and asked, "Conti, can we have a word with you when you're done here?"

"Give me a minute Tony," Peter answered without introducing his buddies. He didn't want his friends knowing anyone, period.

"Guys. I'll give you a call. I need to talk to these fellas. Later I'll head over to my parent's house. I obviously need to have a serious conversation with them. When it's over, I'll catch up with you at Jake's. I'll call you. I know I'm gonna need a drink."

"Jesus Christ All Mighty," spewed Ray.

"This is fuckin crazy Peter," was the comment of the obviously upset Sonny Lippa.

"OK, buddy. Just call us. We'll be there. We'll always be there for you. You know that," responded Al.

The three friends got up to leave and nodded to the three strangers as they left the restaurant.

"Who are those guys boss?"

"Guys under my protection. Protection from everybody and I mean EVERYBODY. You've seen their faces. I want you to remember them."

"Yeah Peter. No problem," replied Tony. "So, what's up?"

"I need everybody here tomorrow morning around 10 AM. I want to make sure we're all on the same page about the Canada thing. And, it's time for a new plan. I'm not Vito. Nobody could ever be. Things are gonna be different. I want a meeting."

"You got it Conti."

"Oh, Tony, good job on the black-market stuff."

"I just did what you told me to do Boss. You're the man. The whole crew knows the score and backs you all the way. You know that, right?"

"That's good news. What you need to know is killing ain't my thing. Making money is."

"Yeah sure. Whatever you say Conti, BUT."

"NO BUTS. The Flower Man is gone. You got that. All the men need to know that too. The only way the Flower Man comes out of retirement is if someone forgets that."

"Everybody will be here tomorrow. Count on it."

"What I count on is you, Tony. I know you'll take care of things. Vito told me he trusted you all the way. I will too. Never doubt that."

Tony, Vic, and Nino left with smiles on their faces. Every man in the crew knew things would be different under Peter Conti. One thing was running through all their minds when it came to their new boss, they were all going to make a lot more money. Remember, they just wiped out the Russian Mob under Conti's rule. To the victors go the spoils.

Peter Conti was the man.

Chapter 3

MAFIA, LLC
The Conti Story Continues

Peter walked through the back door of his childhood home and found, waiting at the kitchen table, his father Tom, his mother Theresa, his brother Russell with his wife Colleen, and his little sister Marie.

"Oh oh, Peter thought."

Peter spoke first, "Hey guys, what's up? We haven't had a meal together in a while."

"What's up are exactly the right words," said his dad quite firmly.

"What do you mean?"

"Jesus Christ Peter. What the hell are you doing?"

"I came here to see my family and all of a sudden I'm on trial."

His mother calmly said, "Honey, you've quit your job, you're moving out of your house, and you own a restaurant. Not just any restaurant, the Delaware Grill. Don't you think we need an explanation?"

"We're just worried Bro," added his brother Russ.

Marie got up from her chair and just hugged her big brother.

"OK, you all want to know, OK, I'll tell you. It's something I should have told you years ago. It's about Vito Bansano."

"Jesus Christ Almighty!" exclaimed Tom.

"Hold on dad. Let me finish. This is not what you think at all. Peter went into the same explanation he just gave his friends, but it was vitally important that he did. Vito Bansano was a good man to me, a very good man. It all started when I was just a young man, a kid for crying out loud. Back when I was going to college. I didn't know anything about him or his reputation when I went into that restaurant. The restaurant was close to school, that's all, and the food was good. What can I tell you? After a while the owner, Vito, came over, probably to check me out, I guess. We talked. That's it, we talked. You know, I never had a grandfather. Both your dads died when I was young. He was a grandfather figure to me. He came from the same area in Italy as our family and he told me all about growing up there. I enjoyed our talks. We became friends. When it became obvious to him that he was putting me in, call it, an awkward position he asked me to stay away. He said it for my own good, BUT he told me straight out to not come back. He wasn't the kind of guy who made friends. He made a point of that, but he said it was too late. He was my friend and he was a good friend to have."

"Wait. You knew he was in the Mafia. No, not in the Mafia, the head of the Mafia, and you still went there?" said his father shaking his head in disbelief.

"Will you please let me finish?"

"Of course, I didn't know, or at least when I first met him I didn't, and by the time I figured it out, I didn't care. He was a good man to me is all I knew. I did nothing wrong."

"No one said you did anything wrong sweetheart. We just don't understand any of this."

"Let me tell you all about Vito Bansano. What kind of man and friend he was to me. It says everything about Vito Bansano and my relationship. I never told anyone except Jackie about this until today, but now it's definitely the time for all of you to hear. Dad, do you know why you're alive today? I mean really, alive, not dead. You're alive because of Vito Bansano. That's why. When you had your heart attack, we all sat in the hospital waiting for a miracle. There was no miracle coming dad. You were going to die. But all of a sudden, the most renowned surgeon in the field shows up and performs a quadruple bypass on you. An operation that only a few surgeons in the world were capable of doing and bottom line, you live. Oh, what a miracle. That wasn't a miracle. That was Vito Bansano calling in a favor. When that happened, I figured I'm screwed. He owns me now. But I didn't care. My father was alive and whatever Vito wants from me he gets. You know what he said when I went to thank him and find out the cost? He said I owed him nothing, that's what friends do. What he did had nothing to do with HIS JOB. I was his friend and he wanted to help. There's more. I invited the man to our wedding. He said NO. Why? He said him being there would disrupt the ceremony and there is no way he wanted to take the attention off of us. You know what though, I saw him sneak in and out of the church, unseen. He just wanted to be there. I cared for the man and he cared for me. I don't care what his job was. When he died, I was heartbroken. You think I knew he was going to leave the restaurant and a bunch of money and a lot more to me. I didn't have a clue. But he did. He also left some instructions he would like me to carry out for him. One of them is to take his ashes to Italy and drop them in the Mediterranean off the Amalfi Coast in Sorrento. I already have my ticket. The rest is personal. I owe the man. We all do."

"Why didn't you tell us this before son?" asked his mother.

"For this very reason, mom. Look, I know I'll be under scrutiny. Owning the Delaware Grill will put that on me. But I don't care. This is where I am now. I'm looked at like I'm Vito Bansano's grandson for all intent purposes and I will honor his wishes."

"Is that who you are now? The hell with us?"

"Jesus dad, that's not what I said. What I said is that I will be looked at by the world that way."

"This is ridiculous," continued his dad.

"Look, I'm not going into numbers, but he left me a bunch of money dad. A bunch and a lot more than just money. Why can't you be happy for me?"

"BLOOD MONEY!"

"I'm leaving. I can't talk to you."

Peter turned to walk away with his mother reaching for his arm to stop him. He turned to her and said, "Sorry Mom," and he walked out the door. Russell followed Peter out.

"Don't let dad drive you away Pete."

"Don't worry Russ. He's just upset, and I don't blame him. The thing is, my brother, my life has changed. It changed when Jackie died. You know that. Let me settle into whatever that is. Nothing has changed here with you guys. I love you all with all my heart. That has to be enough right now."

"Man, what a brother God has given me, is all I can say."

"One that loves you is all you need to know."

"I love you too."

"I know. Now, try and keep him calm. I'm not gone. I just have stuff I have to take care of. I'll stay in touch Russ. See you later."

"Bye Peter."

Peter left the house with a sad heart and headed to Jake's for something to eat and a meet up with his friends. His heart got even heavier as he turned the corner to the site of Jackie's childhood home. The memories surged through him filling his whole being with misery, reestablishing just how he got himself in the position he's in. Not regretting what he's done, just regretting the reason.

His three friends sat silently waiting for Peter to talk. After a few moments, Peter said,
"Here's the thing guys, Vito had numerous investments and legitimate business dealings. I know who he was; I'm not negating that fact. He did not stipulate that I should take over his role concerning the, call it, shady side. I swear to God he never asked me to do that. What he did leave me, in his will, was most of his holdings and most of his assets. In return, he asked me for certain favors."

"What favors?" asked Sonny. "That's what we're all concerned about buddy."

"Personal stuff like his ashes and things of that nature. AND he wanted me to have and take care of his business holdings, including the restaurant."

"What about the guys that hang there? Everyone in the city knows who and what they are."

"You tell me Sonny. Am I supposed to tell them to get out? Look, they don't bother me. What they do with their lives is none of my business. I get along with them and they get along with me. I guess Vito made sure of that, so, if it isn't broke, then why fix it."

"This is crazy shit, man," injected Sonny.

"I'll tell you what crazy shit is. Better yet, I'll show you. Vito not only left me the restaurant, he left me his house too. Guys, it's on Nottingham."

The most elite and luxurious homes in the city of Buffalo are in a small area near Delaware Park. Nottingham is one of the streets in that deluxe neighborhood. You can't even call them homes, they're mansions.

"What? You got a house on Nottingham?" spouted Ray.

"I haven't even seen it. You guys want to go?" asked Peter.

"Sonny, you're right. This keeps getting more and more crazy by the minute. But Peter, we're in. Let's go see how rich you are, buddy," said Al.

Chapter 4

MAFIA, LLC
The Conti Story Continues

The four friends were in near shock as they pulled around the corner onto Nottingham Avenue and saw Peter's new home. Spectacular is a word that would come to mind. It wasn't a house; it was a mansion. All the mansions in the area were built around the same time. They were constructed in the Delaware Park area, very close to the site where Buffalo hosted the Pan American Exposition (the Worlds Fair) of 1901. They were all extravagant homes and a showcase for the city.

"Oh my God," said Ray smiling as he said it.

Peter stopped in front of the wrought iron gates that bordered each end of the half circle driveway that lead to the house. He punched in the code and drove to the front entrance leading up to, the grandiose set of entry doors. On either side of the flight of steps was a concrete lion's head that looked like the MGM lion from the movies. The lion heads overlooked an impressive oversized fountain, situated in the middle garden in the area created by the circle driveway.

Peter stood, mouth open, as he gazed upon the extraordinary structure.

"Millions! The man left you millions," was all that Sonny could say.

"It seems nice," responded a smiling Peter.

Al punched him in the arm and said, "NICE!"

Ray added, "I'd like to say something, HOLY SHIT!" "Who did you have to kill to get this?"

"Bad choice of words, buddy, answered Peter. Remember whose house this is."

"It's your house now Pete. Unbelievable!" said Sonny.

"Anybody want to go inside?" joked Peter.

All three guys laughed at the question. Peter entered the security code and, before you knew it, they were standing on the marble foyer floor looking up at a crystal chandelier the size of a small house. The giant fixture was hanging in the middle of two half-circle stairways leading up to the lavish upper foyer. It was absolutely majestic.

They toured the rest of the house in awe of their surroundings. It was magnificent to say the least.

"Jesus H. Christ, Peter. This place is enormous. How do you plan on paying the heating bill for crying out loud?" asked Sonny.

"Well, Vito also did leave me a few dollars. Let me put it this way. I really never have to worry about money or work another day for the rest of my life."

"Then why keep the restaurant?" asked Ray.

"Because Vito asked me too," replied Peter. "Guys, I told you my life has changed in many ways. I never in my wildest dreams thought it would be like this. But it happened. Believe me, I would rather be in my house with Jackie than here, but that can't be."

"Vito Bansano must really have liked you buddy," said Al facetiously.

"Pal, I'm pretty sure he loved me. He told me many times I was the son he never had. And to be honest, I loved and respected the man as well. He kept our relationship quiet, completely for my sake, that's what kind of man he was," confided Peter.

"Sometimes in life, shit happens."

"Well, I'm bringing Rose here. She has got to see this," injected Sonny about his wife.

"Of course but let me make sure this place is safe before I have a lot of visitors. Vito had enemies you know."

"What do you mean? Are you in any danger, buddy?" asked Ray.

"Naaah. I can take care of myself. But this is all so strange and different and I just want to check everything out."

Sonny responded with, "Here comes the Green Beret stuff."

"No. Just better safe than sorry. Just give me a few weeks to feel things out and then I'll have a housewarming party. People just have to understand; a very rich man left me his fortune, that's all that happened. I'm still the same guy."

"What about your old man?" asked Sonny.

"Time will tell. I doubt if he will even show. He thinks I'm in the Mafia now."

"A lot of people will think that," added Al.

"Let them. I don't care. I can't stop people from thinking what they're going to think. I'm still me. But I'll tell you this guys, this style of living isn't going to be all that hard to get used to. All I can say is Welcome to The Conti Mansion."

The next morning Peter was in his office at the restaurant as the crew gathered for a meeting. All the made men in the Bansano Family, now the Conti Family, were there. Each of these men had soldiers who were under them, but those people do not attend meetings like this. Tony Sotto, Peter's under boss and right-hand man had gathered the men as Peter had asked and everyone was anxious to hear what the new Don, PeterConti had to say. Before the meeting started, Tony asked Peter to come over to meet someone. With the loss of the Gatta brothers, Tony brought up the guy who he wanted for the crews new "Cooler." A cooler, for the lack of a better explanation, is someone they use to put people on ice. The company hitman.

"Peter Conti, this is Joe Gagino. He made his bones a while back and he is a big part of my team. He can be very useful in many ways."

"Hello Joe. Any friend of Tony's is a friend to all of us."

"Hello. Not to be rude, but who the fuck are you?"

With that said, Peter stuck his thumb into Gagino's throat nearly incapacitating the man. Joe reached for his injured neck with one hand and, with the other, started to reach inside his jacket to his shoulder holster for his gun. Peter immediately kicked him in his chest and sent him flying onto a table and then on the floor. Peter then grabbed a fork from the silverware setting sitting on the table next to him and, before Gagino could pull his gun out, he threw the fork and stuck it, in Joe Gagino's hand, like Jim Bowie throwing a knife at a bullseye. Most everyone pulled their guns and they were all pointed at Gagino in seconds.

Tony Sotto reached down and grabbed Gagino by his shirt and screamed at him, "What the fuck do you think you're doing?"

"I was trying to impress the guys here. Who is this guy?"

"He's the boss you stupid motherfucker. He's the Don. The Godfather!"

Gagino's eyes got the size of saucers as he realized he probably only had a few more seconds to live.

Peter coolly reached down and grabbed Gagino's other hand, the one that didn't have a fork sticking out of it and pulled the man up.

"Put your guns away boys. Joe here just made a mistake."

"I'm sorry Godfather. I'm so sorry. I don't know anybody except Tony here and I was trying to make an impression on everybody."

"I'm going to forgive you this time Joe. I don't have time for this shit anyway. But just so you know, next time you talk to me like that, I'LL KILL YOU."

That's how his first meeting as the Godfather got started, an auspicious beginning to be sure. Peter Conti had two personas; one the loving family man and friend and the other, well you just saw it.

That incident actually worked out well for Peter. It re-established just what kind of a man he was in his men's eyes and put an exclamation mark on his position and how he got it.

"Tony. Have a talk with your man. If you think he fills the position you want for him, I'm OK with it. I trust you; you know that."

Peter started the meeting by explaining in a somewhat threatening way how they acquired the Russian business. The demise of the Russian Syndicate was to be completely privy to the people in that room and that a severe penalty would be paid if any information leaked out. He followed up that line of thinking with; The Flower Man is dead and gone. He would only return for one reason, and one reason only, and Peter made it clear that the reason would be detrimental to whomever the Flower Man would be forced to meet. The identity of the Flower Man was sacred and, if ever divulged the perpetrator would not live long enough to enjoy his reward. He looked them all in the eye when saying that and followed that up with a question. "Did I make myself perfectly Clear?"

After saying that, Peter got right into business mode. He had a well laid out map of territories. He had everything broken up for each of his earners, by lists. Lists of their cliental, new and old, their income, contact people, and the police who shared in some of the take. He was adamant about running everything like a business and told his men he was working on a strategic and marketing plan for each and every company, business, and or piece of pie they had their fingers in. He explained how this wasn't a strong-arm situation anymore. He wasn't Vito and he wasn't going to run the organization like he did. The people, cliental if you will, who they all worked with, would all benefit from new business tactics and the protection money they gave to this organization would come back to them in spades by using and implementing the new business plans. It wasn't about breaking arms anymore. It was about business. Working with Peter's organization would make them money and not cost them.

The meeting ended. Most of the men were thrilled knowing firstly they had increased their revenue stream by adding the Russian business to their own and secondly the more their people made, the more they make. I say most because not all of these men are what you would call educated businesspeople. It sounded to them like a whole new world. A world they were not really connected to. They were more used to the breaking heads method of business. Peter assured the group that what he proposed would work and that they would make more money. They could come to him anytime and he would lay out what they should say and how to say it. In the end, everyone was to be on the same page.

It was a new era. The Peter Conti era and everyone would win.

Chapter 5

MAFIA, LLC
The Conti Story Continues

Peter now needed to fulfill one of Vito's wishes and carry out a couple more of his instructions. There weren't many, but Peter was planning on completing every task on the list. Yes, Vito Bansano was the head of a Mafia family and carried out his high position with all his might. That was obvious to all that knew him but the other side, the caring, nurturing, yes loving side Vito had shown to Peter was the reason Peter was on his way to Italy.

Peter stepped off the plane, in Rome Italy, with a smile on his face. It was a beautiful city, filled with undeniable history and near unequaled works of art. He rented a car and his first stop was the Colosseum, also known as the Flavian Amphitheatre. The structure is situated in the center of the city. It was built between 70 and 80 AD and holds up to 80,000 people. Peter was in awe of the place where the historic gladiators fought and died.

From there he visited the famous Trevi Fountain, the most spectacular fountain in Rome. His next stop was to the Vatican City, home of the Pope, to see St. Peter's Basilica. From there off to the Apostolic Palace to view the magnificence of the Sistine Chapel painted by Michelangelo. Peter enjoyed every minute in the country of his ancestors. His only wish was that Jackie could have been by his side.

After two days of sightseeing it was time for the business at hand. He needed to go south towards the Amalfi Coast to the City of Sorrento, the place of Vito's birth. As requested, he was to spread Vito's ashes into the Mediterranean near Vito's childhood home. There was one more thing that Vito, in his will, asked of Peter. He requested that Peter visit Gino Bansano, Vito's brother there in Sorrento.

Peter arrived late in the evening and went directly to the plush villa he had reserved. It was all he could have wished for, especially the marvelous view of the Mediterranean Sea. He rested a few days just enjoying the beauty of the entire area. Peter had no trouble finding Gino Bansano. He owned and operated one of the finest restaurants in the city situated on a point jutting out into the sea. What a beautiful place.

Peter had learned enough Italian from his grandmother on his father's side to get by, but let's just say it was broken Italian at best.

"Excuse me," he said to the maitre d' standing in the front of the exquisite restaurant called Bella Vista (Bella Vista in Italian means beautiful view). "Is Mr. Bansano here?"

"Who may I ask is asking?" the man questioned in Italian.

Peter understood the word who and answered, "Peter Conti, a friend of Gino's brother Vito."

"Una momento."

Gino Bansano who was the spitting image of his brother came out with his hand sticking out to greet his brother's friend.

In near perfect English Gino said, "Hello Peter. My brother mentioned you to me many times over the years. So much so I think of you as my nephew. Please come sit. Let's talk."

"It is a great pleasure to meet you sir. I am amazed by just how much you look like your brother."

"Yes, but a much younger version, right?" he jested.

"Of course, I should have said that first," Peter said with a smile.

Peter added, "I am so sorry that I have to meet you under these circumstances. I am very sorry for your loss."

"My brother's lifestyle was one that this kind of meeting was expected, but not hoped for. I loved my brother and will miss him until the day I die. We didn't see each other much over the past 30 years or so, but still he was my brother."

"Just know his last thoughts were about you sir or I wouldn't be here."

"Thank you, Peter. That gives me some joy knowing that."

With that said Gino waved over a waiter. "Let me feed you Peter. I will join you in a meal."

"Very kind of you sir."

"The name is Gino to my friends so please call me Gino."

"Thank you, Gino. I will, but I'm having a hard time not calling you Vito. You two look so much alike it's uncanny."

"I don't know if that's a good thing or bad."

"Handsome and sophisticated. I think a very good thing."

"Then we will drink some wine to celebrate your kind words."

Gino turned to Paolo, the waiter and said, "Paolo bring us a bottle of the Ravello and two glasses please. What would you like to eat my friend?"

"I'll have what you order."

"Paolo, apetta un minuto, due Tuta Marie, per favore."

"Linguine with sea food?" asked Peter.

"My favorite. I think you will like it my friend."

They ate and drank for hours. Peter felt like he was talking to Vito the entire time. The comfortable conversation was shear pleasure to Peter. He missed his friend/grandfather figure and Gino was nothing short of a remarkable replacement.

"How long are you staying Peter?"

"That brings up the subject I was trying to avoid. I have Vito's ashes with me. He wanted me to give them to you and for you to spread them in the Mediterranean Sea. I hope you will give me the honor of standing by your side when you do."

"Of course. We have some family here that would like to be there as well if you don't mind."

"Mind! That is a privilege to me."

"How long did you say you were staying?"

"As long as you want or need me to stay."

"Good. I will put a little thing together for a nice breakfast with the family, maybe Saturday, and then we will wish my brother a deserved farewell. Until then, please be my quest in my home."

"Thank you, Gino, but I'm already settled in at a villa I rented. But I hope we can spend time together."

"I am at your disposal. I look forward to it. What is your plan for this afternoon?"

"I have no plans."

"You do now. I have a small yacht docked nearby. Let me show you the Amalfi Coast from the water. It's breathtaking."

"It sounds like you are a very successful man."

"Yes, thank you, I do well. But my brother has taken care of me in life and in death. I am comfortable."

"He's done the same for me. He was a good man. And the answer to your kind offer is, hell yes!"

They met that afternoon and spent the rest of the day together. Gino's wife Sofia and his daughter Angelina were aboard. The two women were extremely kind to Peter and if not for Jackie being imbedded deeply in Peter's soul, Peter would have at least asked Angelina to dinner. The cruise was perfect. The coastline was magnificent, and the company was wonderful. Peter was delighted to be in their company and thrilled that in just one day, he was being treated like family.

"I am amazed at the fact that Vito had spoken to you about me," said Peter to Sofia. The women did not speak English as well as Gino, but they did have enough knowledge of the language not to feel completely left out of the conversation.

Gino answered for his wife, "Speak about you. He spoke about you so often I thought he had adopted you. My friend your exploits in the war were his favorite subject. Peter you were the closest thing to a son to my brother and we were all so happy about it."

"He was always so good to me. I feel like I didn't give him enough of my time."

"He knew he couldn't be in your life the way he wanted and yet he followed your every movement. Not like a detective would follow, more like just absolutely interested in your life. When you were honored with all the medals for bravery, he was ecstatic."

"I just did what any man would have done under those circumstances."

"No, my friend. A Silver Star, a Bronze Star, a Purple Heart, and the impressive Distinguished Service Cross, the second highest military award just beneath the Congressional Medal of Honor. Peter you are way too modest."

"How in the world did you know that?"

"Vito. He told everybody in the family about it, many times. I don't think you understand Peter, you are family to us."

"Vito has honored me and now you and your family have. I don't know how to thank you for such a privilege."

"You already have, just by being here and doing this for my brother. You have made us all happy. Because of Vito's business in America, we could not visit. He would not let us. He said it was not safe. He came home often, though and when he did, he spoke of you every time. We were all saddened by the loss of your wife. Vito was heartbroken for you. When he called to tell me about it, he cried. That is not like my brother. He was a very hard man. But not when it came to you."

"I wish he would have told me this when he was alive. Now it seems too late."

"He never wanted you in his life that way. He couldn't. He cared too much about you to put you in danger. He loved you from afar."

"At least I'm here to say goodbye," said Peter solemnly.

"There is great sadness in the loss of my brother but happiness that we got a chance to meet you. I told you, to us, you are family."

"I promise you this will not be the only time you see me. One thing I have always lived my life by is that I treat people the way they treat me. I feel affection coming from you and your family and I will return that and more, Uncle Gino," Peter said with a smile. "Is that OK if I call you that?"

Gino Bansano kissed Peter on both cheeks and said, "Welcome to the family."

Peter spent the rest of his time in Italy with the Bansano family and enjoyed the entire experience. The closeness the family showed each other was noticed at every turn. His trip to Vito's home was absolutely enjoyable to Peter in every way, up until the last day. The day Gino spread Vito's ashes in the sea.

The Bansano family had a service at the church and then all headed to Bella Vista for a funeral breakfast, but first things first. At the foot of the waterfront restaurant, where the Mediterranean Sea washed up on the shore, the family watched as Gino laid Vito's ashes to rest in the beautiful blue water.

Peter cried.

Chapter 6

MAFIA, LLC
The Conti Story Continues

Peter touched down in America with a new lease on life concerning Vito Bansano. Vito went from a very nice man in Peter's eyes, to family. Peter's experience in Sorrento, Italy was life changing in many ways, but the main thing the trip did for Peter was to make him absolutely comfortable in his new house. He had mixed feeling before the trip. He thought he was staying in someone else's home, but after hearing how Vito felt about him, he decided it was an honor living in that mansion. It was Vito's will, not just words in his paper will; Vito's wish was that Peter have what he gave him. Before the trip Peter felt non-deserving now, he felt honored and closer to the man than ever before. Vito gave Peter one more thing and the most important thing of all, a wonderful extended family in Italy.

Peter had decided the minute he stepped on the plane home that he would stay in close touch with his new Uncle Gino and his newfound family. He decided one more thing; he was going to make sure, even though they didn't appear to need it, that he would support them financially. Yes, Vito took care of them in his will, of course, but Peter would make sure they wanted for nothing.

With a new feeling in his heart about his fabulous new mansion, Peter decided it was time for the housewarming party he told his buddies about. But first it was back to his real family for another talk.

"Oh God Peter, I am so happy to see you," said his mother as he walked through the door.

She hugged and kissed him and said, "I was afraid your father drove you away from us."

"Don't be silly Mom. Dad was just being dad. Is he here?"

"No, but your brother is. He's in the bathroom."

"That's more information that I needed," Peter said laughing.

His mom laughed too. Russell walked into the room with his mom and brother still laughing and said, "What's so funny."

"Nothing bro, I'm glad to see you."

"Me too Pete. How was Italy?"

"Oh yeah, I almost forgot you went there. How was it sweetheart?"

"That's kind of why I came here. It was spectacular. The country was beautiful, but the people were amazing. Let me explain and I hope when I'm finished you will understand how everything that's happened to me concerning Vito Bansano and all that he left me came about."

"All ears son."

"Well, I told you about how we first met and how he kind of watched over me from then on, really until he died. And I kind of inferred that he was, in fact, a grandfather figure to me. He was a good man. I don't care what he did for a living; I truly cared for the man. To me, he was a successful businessman and how he went about doing business had nothing to do with what I'm telling you now. What I didn't know until I met his fantastic family in Italy was the depth of the feelings and respect Vito had for me. His brother Gino, what a wonderful man, filled me in. Vito had no family of his own over here. He was a loner and never got close to anyone, Gino said, until me that is. I don't know what I did for the man to feel the way he did about our relationship. I guess it was all the nice talks we had, but to him, I was the son he never had. Gino told me that. Vito constantly informed them of the good things that happened in my life. He reported to the family like he was bragging about his own son, every time they talked. Everything, the Green Beret stuff, the medals, Jackie and my marriage, my business success, everything I've accomplished in my life. The people over there knew me Mom. Gino told me that they considered me family. It changed how I feel about everything. Especially Vito's will. I was confused about it before, but I'm not confused anymore. I'm grateful and I plan on enjoying all of it. Believe me, you have no idea what and just how much he left me, but you will. I'm having a housewarming party Saturday evening. It's not really a housewarming; it's a mansion warming party. Mom, when you see the place you won't believe it. I'm just going to say this straight out, I'm rich."

"Holy shit," exclaimed Russ!

"Russell!"

"Sorry Mom."

"Tell me more Bro."

"I think you'll understand Russ in a few minutes, right after you call your wife Colleen. Give her a call right now."

"What are you talking about?"

"Just call her and give me the phone."

Russ called his wife and handed Peter the phone.

"Hi Colleen. It's Peter."

"Hi Peter. Is something wrong?"

"No Col, everything is great. I'm sure Russ told you that a rich man left me a bunch. Well, it's a big bunch, so Russ listen up to what I'm telling your wife. I love your little apartment and I know you guys are saving up for a house, but just use that money for something else cause

85

I'm giving you a belated wedding present. I'm handing Russ the keys to Jackie's and my house. I'll get you the deed when I see you guys Saturday and there's no mortgage. I love you both and I want you to enjoy it."

"Oh my God. Thank you, thank you, thank you Peter, but."

"No buts. I'm thrilled to do it. Really Colleen, enjoy."

Russell hugged his brother the same way he did when Peter came back from Vietnam.

"Just show up Saturday. I want you to see my new place. It's mind boggling," he told his brother.

His mother kissed him and said, "God has blessed me, son."

"No Ma, God has blessed me and I'm just sharing. I've got to go now, but two things more. Dad, he's got to understand what happened here and not be crazy about it. I hope he comes Saturday, but I'm never sure. Second, I've got a brand-new Cadillac parked outside. Vito gave me a number of cars. Here's a set of keys for it. Give them to Marie and tell her it's a gift from her big brother and she can pick it up when she comes to the party. I don't want her to get pissed cause I gave Russ a house," he said laughing.

Peter sat on the steps of the front entrance as his family and friends showed up. He just wanted to see the looks on their faces. First to drive up were Sonny and his wife Rosey.

"OH MY GOD!" said Rosey.

"You ain't seen nothing yet," said Peter as he hugged his lifelong friend and shook Sonny's hand. "Go inside, I'll be there in just a few minutes. I'm just enjoying the look on everyone's face as they pull up."

"We're going to sit here with you," said Sonny. "You can show Rose around when you give the tour to everyone else. I want to see your mother's face, too."

It wasn't but a couple of minutes later when Peter's dad's car pulled up. Russ jumped out before the car even came to a dead stop, followed by Marie and Colleen and then Peter's mom and dad.

The look on their faces was priceless. His mom started crying.

"Come on in. It's real nice inside," smiled Peter.

Russ just laughed.

Peter's dad said, "I had no idea."

"Just enjoy the ride dad. Come on in."

Colleen walked over to Peter and kissed him a thankful kiss and said, "All I can say is thank you."

"All I can say is your welcome and come on in."

Marie chimed in and said, "Where's my car?" And then hugged her big brother and whispered in his ear, "I love you Pete. I'm so happy for you."

Peter grabbed his mother's hand and said to everyone, "Come on, let me show you around. It's a trip and welcome to my home."

The rest of the people showed up and the same scene was repeated over and over.

When everyone was leaving, Peter's father pulled Peter aside to talk.

"Son, I'm happy for you, but I'm concerned, and I think you know why."

"Dad, I'm a big boy. I know what I'm doing. Everything in life comes with a price. I know that. But I can handle anything that comes my way."

"Peter."

"I can handle it, Dad."

Thomas shook his head and hugged his son. "I hope you know what you're doing."

As they left, Peter realized tomorrow was another day. Back to the restaurant and back to the business at hand. Tonight, he was the son. Tomorrow he's **The Godfather**.

Chapter 7

MAFIA, LLC
The Conti Story Continues

Peter walked into a covey of his men sitting around having coffee.

"What's going on?" he asked as he stopped at their table.

"All good shit, Boss," answered Tony Sotto.

"Like what?"

"Like the business is flowing and nobody's getting killed."

"That's what I like to hear," said Peter

Vic Desica piped in, "The White Cab Company, they are very happy with your advertising plan thingy, Boss. The two Brokaw brothers were starting to give me trouble last year and I was thinking I was going to have to break some heads, but with this advertising business plan working, they're as happy as larks. Revenue is flowing in from the sale of the ads and their profits are soaring and so is our end."

"I knew that would work. They weren't carrying any advertising on their cabs at all, cabs that drive around the city for all to see. Now they put some ads on them, get a nice price for the ads and just like that, more money for everybody," commented Peter.

"Yeah, like I said Boss, they're happy."

Vito Sordi added, "I got three guys who've been putting ads on the cabs and their business is growing from it. Happy people Boss, and, of course, when they do better, we do better."

"You guys are starting to get it? Why extort money when you can earn it. They have partners now, us, but it don't cost them. They make more than it costs. It's a Win."

"Yeah, win," added Tony. "Hey Boss, how did that thing in Italy go. Did you take care of business over there?"

"It went really well. It wasn't business to me. Vito's family is good people. He's resting where he wants. Let's just call it that."

Peter walked back to his office. Tony followed him.

"Boss, you still pissed at Joe Gagino?"

"I was never pissed. I didn't know the guy. I told you, you decide who you can trust. I trust you."

"I'm using him. He's smart. Maybe not when he met you, but he's smart. He can get things done and not bring the shit back here on us. I wanted you to know that."

"OK, you made a decision. I just hope it doesn't come back and bite you in the ass."

"I don't think so. One more thing Boss. This business stuff, at first the guys were thinking, what the fuck, now, we got a lot of happy earners working for us. A lot. All is good."

"Good. Good. Like I told you before, we're just getting started."

As they spoke, Nino Terrisi stuck his head in the doorway and said, "Boss, Antonio Scavazzo is here to see you."

"OK Nino tell him I'll be with him in a second. Anything else Tony?"

"No, Boss."

"Tell Antonio to come in and shut the door behind him."

Antonio Scavazzo is the owner of one of the most exclusive Italian restaurants in the city. He was a good friend of Vito's for a long time and kept a special table at his restaurant for Vito at all times. Vito introduced Peter to Antonio years ago, but Vito had talked to his friend numerous times about Peter's exploits. So much so Antonio knew immediately who Peter was from the first time they met. Right then Antonio offered Peter the same respect as Vito as far as always having a table for him no matter how busy they were. And they were always busy. He never forgot that promise and Peter had frequented the restaurant many times over the years. Peter and Antonio were friends.

"What can I do for you my friend," asked Peter.

"I need your help Godfather."

"What happened?"

"My daughter. My beautiful daughter was raped. And after the son of bitch raped her, he beat her. Peter, he beat her badly. His name is Bill Jorgensen. We called the cops, of course, but the guy had an alibi and claimed that it wasn't him. He must have some pull in this town, I guess because he owns that big-time restaurant downtown. You know, The Executive, where all the politicians eat. He got off scot-free. My daughter is scarred for her life. I'd beat the shit out of the son of a bitch but I'm an old man. I don't know what to do. I just don't know what to do."

"First Antonio, I was in as soon as you said you needed my help. You didn't have to explain anything else. I will take care of this. Tell your daughter not to worry. It will be taken care of."

"Peter, if the guy dies, the police will blame me."

"There are worse things than dying my friend. I'll take care of it. Ask Tony Sotto to come in here on your way out and don't worry Antonio, you came to the right place. Friends help friends. Take care."

"Thank you, Godfather. Thank you!"

Tony came in immediately after Antonio left, "What's up Boss?"

"Get Joe Gagino in here. I want to talk to him. Plus who has working girls? I need one to put a guy in a compromising position, with pictures. One more thing, I need a shitload of roaches."

"The bugs?"

"Yeah, the bugs. Can you get them from somewhere?"

"I don't know Boss. I never tried."

"Well, get some. But don't bring them around here."

"For what?"

"You know the restaurant downtown called The Executive?"

"Yeah, I know the place."

"I want you to get a bunch of roaches and fill that place. I'll make an anonymous phone call to the Department of Health and we're going to shut the joint down."

"OK, but what about the hooker and Joe?"

"The owner of the joint's name is Bill Jorgenson. We're going to close his business with the roaches and bankrupt the son of a bitch. I want the hooker to make a move on the guy, pick him up, and bed him, and get pictures doing the guy. Let's ruin his marriage too. Once that's accomplished, I want Joe to break both his legs and both his arms."

"You mad at the guy?" joked Tony.

"It's a favor."

A few months later Sonny and Ray went to the Delaware Grill to have lunch with their buddy. As soon as they walked through the door, they were being carefully watched. Joe Gagino had no idea who they were and took special interest in the two men.

"Is Peter in the back?" Sonny asked Joe who was blocking their way to the back office.

"Who wants to know?"

"Joe, these guys are friends of Peter's. He's in his office you guys. I'll tell him you're here," said a congenial Tony Sotto.

Peter walked out of his office with a smile on his face. "Don't you have access to a phone for crying out loud. Where have you guys been?"

"What do you mean? You're the one gallivanting all over the world. How was Italy?" asked Ray.

"Don't change the subject. What, all of a sudden I've got leprosy or something?"

"We're busy, your busy, you know, life," added Sonny.

"We're here now, so you got time for lunch?" asked Ray.

"Absolutely! But not here, I eat here way too much as it is. I know a great Italian place and I'm pretty good friends with the owner. We'll walk right in. You got time?"

"Sounds great. We're in," answered Sonny.

The three friends meandered into Antonio's laughing about something as they did. Antonio Scavazzo greeted them personally at the door.

"Hello Peter and welcome!"

"Thank you, Antonio. How you doing?"

"Better than you can ever imagine. Thank you my friend and I mean for everything."

"That's what friends are for."

"I'm glad you called Peter. Your table is all set up for you and your friends."

"Antonio Scavazzo," he said with his hand held out to the two men accompanying Peter. "Any friend of Peter's is a friend of mine. Follow me gentlemen."

"You ever been here before?" joked Sonny.

Peter laughed.

"Jesus Christ Pete, the guy acts like you're famous," added Sonny.

"Vito, he left him to me, in the will. What can I say? No really, he's a good man and we're friends, that's all. And the food, you're going to start crying when you taste it. I can't believe you've never eaten here before."

"I'm saving up for a car," said Ray. "I can't afford to eat here. You have to be rich or know someone to come to this place."

They ordered a drink and talked a bit before ordering food. Sonny wanted to ask Peter a number of questions about everything but decided it wouldn't be a good idea. Peter had already told him numerous times that he didn't want anybody knowing anything. He inferred that could be extremely dangerous. Sonny was smart enough to just say nothing. Just then, a beautiful young woman walked over to their table.

"Hello Mr. Conti. Do you remember me?"

"Of course, Julie. How are you sweetheart?"

She started to cry and hugged Peter with all her might. "Thank you, thank you. I'm good now. Thank you, Mr. Conti."

"I'm happy you're ok sweetheart. Just knowing you're feeling better is all the thanks I need, but I really don't know what you're talking about," he said as he winked at her.

She kissed him full on the mouth and left.

"What the fuck," said Sonny? "Who," is all he got out before Peter answered?

"That's Antonio's daughter. She's a beautiful girl, isn't she? "She had a bad thing happen and she thinks I helped her out of it, that's all."

"No, you don't. Come on Peter don't leave us hanging. Tell us something," said Ray.

"Look, you're not stupid. I know you have some preconceived notion that I'm more than the owner of the Delaware Grill. I get that. Don't make me say anything, OK. Shit just happens."

"How deep?" asked Sonny.
"Let's just say Vito left me more than his house and leave it at that."

"How deep?" Sonny repeated.

"The tuta marie is great here or the lingune with claims both tremendous."

"OK, I get it," replied Sonny.

"Let's just say I have some pull. That should give you some idea."

"What did you pull to get that beautiful girl out of trouble?"

"This is between us, OK. Seriously, that poor girl was raped and beaten by a son of a bitch who thought he got away with it. He didn't. Let's say I had a few favors owed me. I'll say this much. That fucker is broke, on his way to a divorce, and will walk with a limp for the rest of his life. At least that's what I heard. But what do I know?"

"Jesus Christ, you're in the Goddamn Mafia," said a dejected Sonny.

"NO. Or at least that's all you know. You understand?"

"Are you?"

"I won't say, but the word around town is that I am. Can't you just leave it at that? I'm still Peter, your friend. I just have a little bit different job now. That's all I'm saying."

"How could something like this happen for crying out loud?" asked Ray.

"The fucking Russians killed my wife, that's how. Look, I really don't want you guys to know anything at all about the goings on at the restaurant. That's why I've asked you to stay away. Let me ask you this. Do you think Robin Hood was a bad man? Do you?"

"You're fucking funny. You know that," injected Sonny.

"I'm just careful buddy. Careful enough to say that's the last of this conversation. Let's order and let's eat. Let's enjoy this afternoon. I really miss you guys."

Peter called for the check. Antonio came over and said, "There is no check and there never will be. Thank you, my friend. I owe you."

Peter laid a heavy tip on the table and said, "You owe me nothing but your friendship."

As the three friends walked out, Antonio said, "God bless you Peter Conti. God bless you."

Chapter 8

MAFIA, LLC
The Conti Story Continues

Peter had big ideas to change the focus of what he called a business renaissance in the organization. He called for another meeting to forge ahead with his new plan; a plan to legitimize the entire operation. This time his earners weren't skeptical of what Peter was proposing. They were anxious to hear. Peter had the confidence of each and every one of them. After all, everything he has presented to them before and after he took over has suited their every need. Revenge, getting rid of the competition, and making a lot more money for all of them was the proof in the pudding. Peter Conti was definitely the man and his men were all ears.

"Guys. Do you know what the biggest threat to us is right now?"

Gino Palidino yelled out laughing, "Boss, we don't have anybody threatening us. We do the threatening."

"Wrong Gino. We have a giant threat. It's called the IRS. That's how they got Alfonse Capone back in the day and that's how they can nab us."

"What do you mean Boss?" asked Frankie Nero.

"Frankie, you drive a brand-new Cadillac Fleetwood Brougham. Where did you get the money?"

"What do ya mean? You know where."

"Yeah, I know where, but the IRS doesn't because you don't claim it. That's called tax evasion and that's how they got Capone. So, here's what we're going to do; I'm going to start a legitimate company and call it Zorde International LLC, a consulting group."

Everybody laughed because zorde is the Italian word for money.

"No, I'm not kidding. Here me out. From now on we get checks not cash from our customers, written out to Zorde International. If you get cash, that's fine, no problem. Turn it in like always and we'll divvy it up. I'm pretty sure you don't want the other guys like, Sotto or Gagino, finding out you pocketed without sharing. Those guys are scary. I know I wouldn't want to fuck with their money."

Everyone laughed again, but they understood what Peter was saying, for sure.

"The clients will be able to write off the payment that way, saving them on taxes. They'll love it. I'll divide the money up according to your normal earnings, as usual, and pay you with a check from Zorde International, not cash. This is a big deal because at the end of the year you'll get a W-2 form and you'll have to pay taxes on the earnings. All legal. Yes, of course, that sounds bad now, but it won't if you're doing 10 to 20 years for tax evasion. But understand this, we got plenty of ways to beat a bunch of taxes, called write offs. I know you guys aren't comfortable with a lot of this, but you don't need to know any of this paperwork gamodia (gamodia means stuff in Italian). I got Vito's accountant and lawyer working on the loopholes for everybody. They know everything about the rules and regulation. Just keep making money and they'll take care of the government bullshit. Always keep in mind, we'll be running two sets of books. That goes without saying."

Everyone laughed again.

"But what all this means is no hiding anything. Cars, houses, jewelry, anything you buy becomes legit, and some of it is a write off. We're safe from the IRS and the clients pay less in taxes. Another win-win."

"One more thing. Vito still has investment ties with us along with some of his own money, all still tied up in our organization. It's making money for us and for him. That's where the international comes in. Vito's profits go to his family over there in Italy. If anybody has a problem with that, say it now."

The room was quiet. Vito was not forgotten, and he was still respected by everyone in that room. That was a given.

"OK. Each of us will hold a position in the company. You are all going to be called Area Managers. That's your title in the organization. Your men are your Consulting Reps and will be paid the same way as always, but with checks from the new company, Zorde International. When you tell them all this, explain it the same way I'm explaining it to you. The 10 to 20 years in prison should get their attention and should make everything clear. My title will be CEO. That stands for Chief Executive Officer in our language Godfather," Peter laughed when he said that. "Tony Sotto will be COO, Chief Operations Officer, of course, that means head of operations, understand nothing is changing just what we're calling ourselves. The Treasurer will be the guy Vito had been using for his accountant forever. You all know him, Anthony La Maccia, his title is CFO, Chief Financial Officer. Our lawyer, you all know him too and if you don't that means you've been able to keep your nose clean. His name is Tom Thomas. I don't know what his real last name is, but knowing Vito, he's probably a Jew. Vito always said Jews make the best lawyers. Anyway, whatever it is, I don't give a Goddamn. He might be Jewish, but he acts like he's a Gumba (a close Italian friend), that's for sure. But bottom line, he's good. Anybody got any questions?"

"This is a lot to swallow, Conti," said Tony Sotto.

"Nothing changes Tony. It's business as usual. The only change is accounting. I know what I'm doing."

Alberto Nazzi piped in, "I don't know about the rest of you guys, but I'm doing whatever the Boss says. So far, it's been real good for me."

"Me too," said Frankie Nero.

"Anybody against?" asked Peter.

No one said a thing. "Then Welcome to Zorde International, LLC."

Chapter 9

MAFIA, LLC
The Conti Story Continues

The next morning Peter heard a knock at the front door. It was his brother Russell.

"Come on in Russ. What's up?"

"Nothing. Can't I visit my brother when I feel like it?"

"Of course, anytime. You have any breakfast yet? Hazel was just making me some French toast. You want some? I'm telling you bro Hazel is a God sent, she is without doubt the best cook in the world."

"No Bro sounds great, but I already ate. Some coffee would be nice, though."

"Hazel put a hold on breakfast for a bit and just bring out a pot of the heavenly coffee of yours for me and my brother. Thank you."

"It's good to see you. But don't give me that shit about just dropping by. Russ, I know you, something's up. What happened?"

"Naah, I'm good."

"Bullshit. What happened?"

"I got canned from my job and I haven't told Colleen yet. So, I left home like I was going to work. I don't know what to tell her."

"What the fuck. What do you mean you got canned? Why?"

"I got fired. Let's just leave it at that."

"You've got to be kidding. Let's just leave it at that my ass. Tell me what happened?"

"My boss says to me that Smith, Smith, and Smith is a reputable accounting firm and he was concerned about the fact that you, being my brother, would scare off some of our clientele. So, I told him, go FUCK YOURSELF. He fired me."

"WHAT?" "What's this guys name? Maybe if I slap him in his face a bunch of times he'll come to his senses, cause this guy ain't thinking straight."

"No, Peter. I don't want that. It's just that the whole damn town is talking about you like you're in the Mafia or something. Some people think you're the Godfather for Christ sakes." Russell hesitated before he continued with, "Are you Bro?"

"Goddamn It! I'm really sorry about what happened Russell."

"Answer me Peter. Are you in the Mafia?"

"Let's go into my office. It's in the guesthouse in the back. I don't want any of the help to hear anything about anything."

"There you go. That's just what I mean. Did you just hear yourself Pete? You don't want any of the help to hear you. Jesus Christ Peter, look around. You think we're all stupid. Mom and dad are sick to their stomachs with worry. Marie and Colleen don't know what to think and me, come on Bro, fess up, what's going on?"

"Come back with me. Let's talk."

They walked out of the breakfast room, through the pool area to the guest house/pool house, where Peter had a home office. Needless to say, it was plush.

"Russ, sit down. What I have to say cannot leave this room. Forget about all this materialistic stuff. Here's the thing, let me go over this one more time. Vito semi-adopted me and treated me like I was the son he never had. The man had true affection for me, that's all I can say. He respected me and I gave it right back. When he died, it broke my heart. I guess I did love the man. He was a good man to me. I told you some of this at Mom's. Weren't you listening? Bottom line, he left me everything you see."

"I get that part Peter and I'm happy for that. It's the Mafia thing. People wouldn't talk if it weren't true."

"Look Russ, Vito had his fingers in a lot of pies throughout the city. The truth is everything wasn't quite legal. He left that shit to me, too. I'm trying to legalize it all. And I'm doing it. Let people talk. I don't give a shit. Tell Mom and Dad and the girls don't worry I know what I'm doing. And tell them it's legal. I have a piece of a lot of different companies; he left a lot of shit to me in the will Russ. So, brother let me help you. Just tell me what you want to do? These are all legitimate companies Bro. Just say the word and you'll be working at one of them in the morning."

"That's not why I came here."

"SHUT UP, I'm not listening to you. Just tell me what you want to do? Wait, I got a better idea. How about this? You want to start up your own accounting firm? I'll fund it, no problem. Just say yes and we'll make that happen."

"Peter."

"Don't Peter me. You're an accountant. Go find a location, get some staff and get started. I'm sure you'll be able to keep a number of your personal client base. You're good. Just tell me how much you need, and it's done. PLUS, I just told you; I own a piece of a lot of legitimate companies. This ain't Mafia shit Russ, honest. All legitimate. I'll ask them to use your new accounting firm. You'll be busy in no time. You want some revenge for getting canned from them stupid sons of bitches. Go after their business."

"Peter."

"Stop. You don't have to say anything to anybody about this. Just tell everyone you've been working on getting a loan and it came through. Nobody has to know. If they ask, you've been working with an investment firm called Zorde International. That's all they need to know. I got faith in you my brother. You're gonna do well. This is a good day."

"I love you Peter; you know that don't you?"

"Shut the fuck up. That's what brother's do. You know what? Let's go looking for a good location right now and then over to Antonio's for a nice lunch. I want to help."

"Is that a joke? You want to help? How much more can you do? You are something else my brother. Really something else."

"Let's go. This is going to be fun."

Russell hugged his brother and Peter hugged him right back. Peter had no intension of bringing his brother into any part of his business. He was serious that this was strictly legitimate. He had helped quite a few companies with his new business plan, and he would make it crystal clear he wasn't forcing anyone to use his brother's new accounting firm. He would never put Russell in that position. Russell was a standup guy and honest as the day is long. Peter would definitely let the people he talked to know just that. This was another win-win.

A few days later, Russell invited the family, including Peter, for dinner at his home. He had an announcement that he wanted to make, and he wanted the entire family to hear. Peter was a tad reluctant to accept the invitation for two reasons. One, he was uncomfortable being in his and Jackie's old house. The house held too many memories for Peter and it still hurt. And secondly, he didn't want to have any kind of confrontation with his dad. This was all about Russell and not him, but he knew his dad and he knew saying nothing was not his dad's thing. He went anyway.

Russell made his announcement to a crescendo of applause from the family, led by Peter. Russ explained that he had been working on starting his own business for some time and finally the funding came through. He found a willing investment firm. He explained, but not in detail, that it was a good fair deal on both ends and that he had already picked out the location and everything was in the works. It should be up and running within the month.

"Congratulations son," said a smiling Thomas Conti.

"Thank you, Dad. I've been working on this, but I didn't want to say anything to you guys until I could put the whole deal together, and now I have."

"This is great news my brother. Can I help? How you set for money until it's all up and running?"

"I'm good Peter. But if it takes longer than I had hoped, I'll ask. I'm not shy."

"I mean it Russ. This is not a problem for me. You know that."

"He doesn't need any of that DIRTY MONEY of yours Peter. Russ is a straight up guy," injected their father.

"And I'M NOT. Is that what you're insinuating?"

"I'm not insinuating a thing. I'm saying it outright."

"Goddamn it Dad! Can't you let Russell have his day without bringing up shit you know nothing about?"

"I got ears."

"Well, how about talking to me about it before you accuse me. You don't think I don't hear this shit every Goddamn day of my life?"

"Peter." Thomas started to say something more but was immediately interrupted.

"Stop, stop it right now, both of you," said Theresa loudly. "Peter, we are all concerned with the rumors that are flying around the city. Your father, in fact the whole family, and I have concerns about what we're hearing. Your father is just more vocal about it."

"Mom, I hear the rumors too. And yes, of course, I'm concerned too, but what you're hearing just isn't true. I am not Vito Bansano. Yes, I've inherited a lot from the man, including a number of businesses, but I swear to you I am running everything legitimately. I'm a businessman Mom and a damn good one. I think that's why Vito left them to me. It will take time for me to rid myself of the stigma of being called Vito's prodigy, but I'm not him. It's a lot of business Mom and a lot of money. Why would I throw that all away?"

Thomas came back with, "We all hear what you're saying son, but we have to live with all the talk."

"Its just talk Dad. There's such a thing as being innocent until proven guilty in this country, you know. This whole city has me marked like I'm Al Capone cause Vito left me a bunch of money and property. Why don't you try being proud of me instead of believing everything you hear?"

Theresa answered, "We are proud of you Peter. We always have been."

"I know you have Mom. Thanks," Peter said as he started to push his chair back to leave.

"Damn it Thomas," said Theresa. "Do not drive our son away again!"

"Wait Peter. Your mother is right. I've been jumping to all kinds of conclusions and I'm sorry. It's just that all these rumors."

"Look, all of you. All the rumors are not false. Vito was involved in many suspicious activities. I'm paying the price for that. But I'm telling you I am doing everything I can to legitimize everything. I really am and I'm sorry but a lot of this has to do with Jackie. I'm sorry for a lot of things. I will always keep you out of any of this. I swear. I'm sorry. I think I should go."

"Wait Peter, this is my house and I want you to stay. We love you Peter," said Colleen.

"We all do," added Russell.

"I know and I love you all. And I know you all know that. It's just that these rumors are not going to end for a long time, and I don't want any of you to be harmed because of it. I'm not going to leave the family in any way, but what I am going to do is be somewhat of a stranger. You don't need this, and you certainly don't deserve it. I'm glad we cleared the air. It had to be. I am sorry. Now can we just talk about Russ's new venture and eat? I just want to be with my family right now."

Chapter 10

MAFIA, LLC
The Conti Story Continues

Business was flowing like the Niagara River, fast and furious. Peter's men were selling the concept and the clients were very happy people. Remember, they were paying and getting nothing in return except let's say protection for a long time when they were under Vito's thumb. Now, under Peter, everyone's business was growing, and the tax benefits added a lot more profit to the bottom line. Win, win, win. Russell's accounting firm was thriving and not a dime of it was made illegally. Peter would never allow that.

"Peter, a guy by the name of Tom Kline is here and he wants to see you. He said he's your brother-in-law. I guess he's married to your wife's sister Jill," said Nino Terisi.

"Don't just stand there, tell him to come in here."

"Hey Tommy, come on in. Good to see you. What's up?"

"I'm not sure Pete. To be honest with you, I didn't know what else to do or who to go to."

"What are you talking about?"

"Well the word on the street is that you have a lot of friends in high places, so I was thinking maybe you could help me."

"Spit it out Tom. What happened?"

"I'm not accusing you of anything, you know that, right Peter?"

"Tom, whatever you're talking about doesn't matter. Something happened to you so, tell me what it is."

"OK Peter, here it is. My auto shops are doing pretty good. Thank you, because an awful lot of people tell me you sent them there."

"Yeah, yeah, of course Tommy, you're family. Now get to the point."

Tommy Kline had his hat in his hand and was curling it up as he spoke.

"Tommy, Jesus Christ, what are you doing? It's me Peter you're talking to. What are you so nervous about? We're family for Christ sakes."

"I know Peter, but we haven't really talked for some time and."

"Stop, Tommy, how can I help you?"

"Well, this man. He said his name was Mario Marconi. He came to my shop. The one on Jefferson, and said he had a proposition for me. He said for $500.00 a month he would protect all three of my shops from any harm that might come to them. I threw him out. Last night my tow truck caught fire and burned. I can't say it was him but. I'm scared Pete."

"You said Mario Marconi? What did he look like?"

"He was a big guy, bald on top. He had a tattoo of a snake on his right hand. That's all I know."

"Did he say when he would be back?"

"Yes, he called me this morning and said he'd be by this afternoon around two to see if I changed my mind."

"OK Tommy. Don't be scared brother. I'll come by and have a talk with him when he comes."

"I'm sorry Peter. I didn't want to bother you with this. I'm just scared."

"You came to the right place. I'll come by around 12:30 and we'll go to lunch. It's good to see you. We can catch up. How's Jill and my mother and father in law. Is everyone OK?"

"Everyone is doing the best they can. It's been awhile now, and they say that time heals all wounds, but Jill is still heartbroken. I guess she will be forever, so are Mike and Patti, but I don't think I have to tell you that. I can't even imagine how you feel. I'll tell you this, we all miss you, and you know, that right? We think about you often."

"Yes, I know that Tommy. I miss all you guys too. Tell everyone I said hello. Now get out of here and I'll see you at 12:30."

Tommy left and Peter called for Tony.

"Problem Boss?"

"Maybe. You know a guy by the name of Mario Marconi?"

"No, I don't think so. Wait, I think he's the big mouth that hangs around at the pool hall on West Ferry. He's a wanna be. What about him?"

"Is he connected?"

"No Boss. He's a loner. Why?"

"He's causing me some grief."

"You want me to have Gagino talk to him?"

"No. This is personal. I think I'll handle this myself. I'm gonna talk to the guy this afternoon. I just wanted you to know what I'm doing and with whom."

"You sure Boss?"

"Yeah Tony. This is a family matter. No problem."

Peter met Tommy at the shop on Jefferson Avenue and they went out for a pleasant lunch. It was a little uncomfortable for both at first. Tom because of all the scuttlebutt he's heard about Peter, he just didn't know what to expect. But after a few minutes, Tom realized it was just the same old Peter he had grown to love over the years. Peter was uncomfortable because he just can't stand talking and thinking about Jackie without a great sadness taking over him. That too faded a bit during the conversation. After lunch, they headed back to the shop. Peter told Tom to let him do all the talking.

Mario Marconi walked into Tommy's office with a smug look on his face.

"Who's this guy?" Mario asked.

Peter stood up and started walking towards the guy, "My name is Peter Conti."

With that said, Mario started to reach into his jacket pocket for his heater. Peter grabbed the gun out of his hand and flung it against the wall. He hit Mario so hard in his face that you could hear his cheekbone crack. Peter then drove his fist into the hoodlum's chest and again into his stomach. Mario went down. Peter kicked him in his face 4 or 5 times and not politely. Mario was a mess. Peter picked the man up and got him to his feet and whispered something in his ear and let him stagger out of the office.

"Jesus Mary and Joseph, Peter. I thought you were only going to talk to the man."

"That's the only language people like him understand."

"I'm sorry Peter. I didn't want you to get involved like that. I thought you would just call someone and find out what to do."

"No need Tommy. This man will never bother you again. You have my word."

"Holy shit Bro. We all knew you were a tough son of a bitch, but holy shit."

"Tommy that's the only way you can handle somebody like this. So, it's handled. Do you have insurance on your truck?"

"Yes Peter. No problem there."

"You have another truck to use until you buy another one cause I know some people?"

"Yes Peter. I have back up."

"Then I'm out of here. It was wonderful seeing you again. Come by anytime. My door is always open."

"Jesus Christ. I still can't believe what I just saw. The guy pulled a gun Pete."

"Yeah, that didn't work out too good for him. All he did was make me mad."

"I don't know how to thank you."

"No need. You're family. Tommy, all the shit you're hearing about me ain't all true. The truth is I knew Vito Bansano as a friend, a good friend. Don't listen to everything you hear. But he did leave me a lot of stuff when he died. He left me a beautiful home as well. It's fantastic. If you and the family ever want to come by, you're always welcome."

"Let me say it again Peter, you are missed."

"I miss everyone too. Don't be a stranger."

"Thank you, Peter. You saved my life I think."

"No, he was just a two-bit punk. But I'm glad you came to me. Now it's done."

"Saying thank you just doesn't seem to be enough," said a thankful brother-in-law.

"It is Tommy. You and the family can always come to me for anything. Always, family is family. See you around Tommy."

"Goodbye Peter and thanks again."

As Peter left you could here Tommy in the background say, "WOW!"

Chapter 11

MAFIA, LLC
The Conti Story Continues

Peter left his brother-in-law's shop with feelings of mixed emotions. Any time he thinks about Jackie he's filled with sadness. The kind of sadness that creeps into your soul and just won't let go. The grief overtakes him and is near crippling sometimes. But on the other hand, Peter also truly loved and respected all of Jackie's family. So, seeing Tommy again gave him some pleasure. Helping him out of his situation was rewarding to him. Of course, the fact that Tommy came to him was a sign that not just Peter's immediate family, but Jackie's family as well, thought Peter was connected. The sad thing was they were right.

He needed to do something about the rumors and his reputation.

Peter knew that Vito had made numerous donations of money and time to many charitable organizations. He was on the board of a few of them. Peter needed to take up where Vito left off. But how? He was aware that Vito's main connection to all of the charity stuff was the Mayor of Buffalo, Robert Stonemetz. He decided to drop over to the man's office even though he had two chances of actually meeting with him, slim and none.

"May I help you Sir?" asked the person sitting at the information desk in the front lobby of City Hall."

"I hope so. Is there any chance I can see or set up an appointment to see the mayor?"

"Your name, Sir?"

"Yes of course, Peter Conti."

"Let me ring Mayor Stonemetz's secretary for you. One moment please."

"Thank you," responded Peter.

"You can go up to room 201, second floor. First door on the right, you can't miss it. His secretary's name is Mrs. Marlo."

"Thank you, Sir. I appreciate your help."

"No problem. Have a nice day."

He followed the directions and was standing in front of the mayor's secretary in moments.

"Good afternoon. How may I help you?" asked a very attractive and sophisticated looking Mary Marlo.

"Thank you, yes you can, I'm Peter Conti, Mrs. Marlo, is there any chance the Mayor is free for a five-minute chat?"

"What is this concerning Mr. Conti."

"Contributions to a number of the Mayor's charitable organizations. I am Vito Bansano's representative."

"I'm sure he will put some time on his schedule for a meeting. He makes his own appointments, but I do have his appointment book here. Let's see, it looks like we can fit you in next Monday morning, if that will work for you."

"That's great but since I'm here, is there any chance he can see me now?"

115

"I think not Mr. Conti. I'll ring through but I sincerely doubt it, the Mayor is a very busy man."

She rang the Mayor's phone and, with a look of surprise on her face, said, "He will see you in ten minutes if you have the time to wait."

"That's great. Thank you, Mrs. Marlo."

Ten minutes later a distinguished looking man emerged from his office with his hand held out to shake Peter's.

"Mayor Robert Stonemetz at your service Sir. How can I help you?"

"Peter Conti, Mr. Mayor. The question is how can I help you?"

"Conti, I recognize the name. Are you the war hero Peter Conti?"

"That was a long time ago, but yes Sir, I was in Vietnam."

"Well I'll be, a pleasure meeting you Mr. Conti. May I call you Peter?"

"Of course."

"Come on into my office Peter. Let's talk."

The Mayor sat behind his very large and expensive looking desk and pointed to one of the plush leather chairs situated directly in front of it.

"Vito Bansano was a very good friend to our great city and to me. He was generous with his time and his money, I'm happy to say. Mrs. Marlo mentioned you are the late Mr. Bansano's representative. In what way, may I ask?"

"Sir, Vito Bansano was a great man. Years ago, when I was a kid, he took me under his wing. Upon his death he left me instructions along with many other things. One of his instructions was to follow in his footsteps with his charitable work. He mentioned to me numerous times how he respected you and your efforts in helping those in need.

He said it was a pleasure working with you. I'd like to continue his efforts with both my time and money. How do I do that Sir?"

"First Peter. Call me Bob. Second, I'll put together a list indicating exactly what charities Vito was involved in. Complete with his time and his money involvements. Why don't we have lunch next week? Let me look in my book here. I can't live without this thing. How's Monday?"

"Monday is great. How would Antonio's suit you? I have a private table there."

"That's perfect. I've had lunch with Vito there many times. Shall we say noon?"

"Sounds like a plan. Thank you, Sir. I mean Bob."

"Great see you then Peter. And Peter, I am very sorry for your loss. Vito was a good man. I don't care what the rumors about him were. He was a good and generous man."

"Thanks Bob. See you Monday."

Peter met the Mayor in the parking lot at Antonio's, right on schedule, and they walked in together. A smiling Antonio greeted them at the door.

"Welcome Mr. Mayor and, as always, it's a pleasure seeing you Mr. Conti."

"When are you going to start calling me Peter, Antonio?"

"Starting right now Peter," he said with a big smile.

Just then Julie, Antonio's daughter, walked up and greeted the mayor with a polite "Welcome Mr. Mayor."

The mayor smiled and said, "Thank your young lady."

Julie turned and kissed Peter on the cheek and said, "Hello Mr. Conti. I am always so happy to see you when you come in."

"Julie sweetheart, the pleasure is always mine."

The men were seated and ordered a drink before their conversation even started.

"Peter, I read up on your heroics over there. Wow fella, you certainly served our county with great honor. I was proud just reading the articles."

"Thanks Bob, but when you're over there you just do what has to be done. I don't really like to talk about it. It was just what it was."

"Maybe to you, but not to a grateful America. Thank you, Peter is, all I can say. Although what you did over there will certainly help our efforts when trying to raise money for the kids over at The Children's Hospital. You can bet your sweet ass on that," the mayor said laughingly.

"I hope so Bob. But Vito left me more than just a set of instructions and some of his wealth. He left me holding the rumor mill about him and now those same rumors follow me. It's not a big deal. I'm a big boy. I hope the rumor mill won't interfere in anyway. I can handle the scuttlebutt, but it does hurt my family. That's what bothers me. Just so you know, I don't kill people Bob."

"You mean anymore, Po Jing Pete," he said with a giant smile. "That's what they called you over there isn't it?"

"Yes, how in the world did you know that? I guess that deal over there is going to stick with me for the rest of my life."

"It should. I studied up on all of that and what you did over there. Peter, I learned how and why you were awarded the second highest award given to a combat soldier. I read about it over the weekend.

Here are some facts you just might not know; there were over 9 million military personnel over there in Vietnam. You know how many besides you received the Distinguished Service Cross? 900 and 90 Peter. That is 990 awarded from 1955 to 1975. That's 990 out of 9,000,000. You're a hero my friend. A big-time hero and that fact will definitely go a long way to help our cause."

"I didn't know any of that. All I was trying to do was to save my men."

"That's just what heroes say. Let's publicize that aspect of Peter Conti's life. Vito got some bad press; let's make sure that you don't. I've got a lot of pull with the media my friend. I'll make some calls."

"That sounds real good to me Bob. Real good. I've tried to keep my time in Vietnam private, but, if it can help sick kids, hell with the being private. I'm a businessman, let's make some money for the children."

"That's what I'm saying. It sounds like you're in then?"

"Yes Bob. I'm in."

"OK then. I'll take care of the press right off the bat. This city needs to know who Peter Conti really is. Next, Vito was on the Board of Directors at the Children's Hospital. I still sit on that board and we never did fill his position. Are you interested?"

"Of course. That would be great."

"A sizable contribution will help the cause when I bring you up for consideration."

"How sizable?"

"Are you in a position for a six-figure donation?"

"I can handle that. Will $100,000.00 do it?"

"Absolutely!"

"Count me in. I want to help those kids."

The two men shook hands, ordered food, had a very nice lunch and parted ways with both men accomplishing exactly what they came for.

Mayor Stonemetz has a new and valuable member for his charity committees.

Peter Conti got a renewed lease on life as far as reputation and respect, PLUS a connection in the political world.

WIN, WIN.

Chapter 12

MAFIA, LLC
The Conti Story Continues

It wasn't but three day later when Peter got the call.

"Peter Conti?"

"Yes."

"Could you hold for Mayor Stonemetz please?" asked Mrs. Marlo.

A few seconds later he heard, "Peter, it's Bob Stonemetz. You're in. It was a piece of cake. All I did was show them your news clippings along with the résumé you gave me and said you wanted to help. I mentioned a sizeable contribution but didn't say how much. That's up to you. And "vwa-la" you are on the Board of Directors of the Children's Hospital."

"That's wonderful news Bob. Thank you. I know I can help."

Bob continued with, "I've got a great idea. I was thinking I'd have a get together at my home as a fundraiser AND it would be a perfect time to introduce you. I'm sure some of our heavier contributors would like to meet you; you know the war hero stuff and all. You said let's use it. It's only smart. It also would be an ideal time for you to kick things off with your quite generous contribution. Which will certainly get the ball rolling and no doubt many other contributors will follow. What do you think?"

"Sounds like a wise move. No wonder you were elected Mayor."

"Don't try and sweet talk me soldier, you already got the job."

"Well, I'm not a soldier anymore, but I have heard you can catch more flies with honey."

The Mayor laughed and said, "I find dead squirrels work the best for that."

Both men laughed out loud.

"When are you planning on putting this together?" asked Peter.

"Are you free a week from Saturday?"

"I'm free when you tell me to be."

"Then 7 PM a week from Saturday. I'll send you out a formal invitation along with everyone else's. It will have the address and time and such."

"Great. Can I bring a few quests? My family would get a giant kick out of this."

"Of course. Bring whoever you want. There will be a ton of people there. The more the merrier."

"I'm talking about a half a dozen people or so."

"Wonderful, I'll make sure your family is mentioned on the invitation. In fact, when we're finished with this call, I'll send you back to Mrs. Marlow and you can give a list of whom you would like to invite. I'll have her send all the invitations to you so you can personally hand them out. How's that suit you? I'd love to meet your people. I can use their vote you know."

"Super Bob. What a great call. I won't let you down. Helping sick kids, what better cause is there?"

"That's the spirit. I'll see you then. Take care Peter."

"You too Bob. And thanks again."

Peter hung up the phone with numerous questions running through his mind. Main question, how does he pull off this double life he's leading and get away with it? Then it struck him. Vito was able to do it for almost 30 years. Why can't he? He also came to the realization that, the more he legitimized his operations the easier it would be. He needed a strategic plan. He already put a number of marketing plans in motion, but he needed more. He headed to his office at the Delaware Grill to contemplate his next business-oriented move.

Peter walked in and found Vic Desica waiting for him.

"Hey Boss. I've been waiting for you. I got a problem or at least my guys at the White Cab Company got a problem and they asked if we could help."

"Spit it out."

"Well, there's a new guy in town. He owns the Green Cab Company and he's looking for a location to open up another location. He's looking at the Buffalo market. My guys are scared shitless that it will kill their business. I wanted to get your permission to take care this Greenberg guy."

" Hold off on that Desica. Let me figure something out first."

"OK boss, but like I said, my guys are going nuts on me."

"Let me take care of this. We don't need the cops breathing down our necks just when things are going so good for us. I'll take care of it."

"OK Boss. Whatever you say."

Peter did some research on population and cab usage in the area and put together a presentation showing that the area really couldn't support two cab companies. He drew it up, found that Alex Greenberg was staying at the Ritz, and went there to meet with him.

"What can I do for you Mr. Conti?" said the unsuspecting businessman.

"It's what I can do for you Mr. Greenberg."

"What might that be Sir?"

"Well, I heard through the grapevine that you were here doing some research on the Buffalo market to expand your taxi business here. I had the same idea a year ago and found that it would take 4 years to just get from the red to the black at a 10% profit ratio. That is IF and I mean IF you can take half of the business away from the White Cab Company. Bad odds. I have it all here in a report."

"And what do you want for that information?"

"I was thinking $1,000.00 would pay for my time and save you much more than that. I have the information right here. Are you interested?"

"Well, I like this town."

"Yes, I do too. But I like money better. I have a feeling you do too. Are you interested in buying this report?"

"Not really. I think I can find out what I'm looking for on my own."

"OK. It's your money. I thought maybe I could recoup some of mine by sharing. Now I can wipe my ass with this report. It did what I needed it to do. Up to you, now you're going to spend time and money to find the same results. All I can say is, good luck Mr. Greenberg."

Peter definitely wanted to say something like listen here you motherfucker, if you try and open a cab business in this town, you're going to find bad things happening to your cabs and your drivers BUT he really wanted to take the high road and do this businesslike. Just before he got to that point, he heard.

"I like you Mr. Conti. You're a man after my own heart. You took a chance and found out it was going to be a loser and now your trying to make a little lemonade from some lemons. That's smart and good business. Let me ask you. Are you looking for work?"

"No sir. I have a number of other interests in businesses and I'm doing just fine."

"OK then. I don't know you from a bag of apples, but I think I can trust that report of yours. I haven't had dinner yet. If you haven't and you would like to join me, I think me buying dinner and $500.00 would make both of us happy."

"Dinner and $500.00 for me and a big savings for you. Win, Win."

The men went down to dinner and had a wonderful conversation. Mr. Greenberg went over Peter's bullshit figures and decided it was too much of a risk to try and expand here in this market. Peter swayed the conversation over to Albany. The town is wide open, full of politicians who almost always rode cabs and the start up costs would be much less. Greenberg decided to take his dog and pony show there instead.

Manipulation is better than breaking heads. Peter Conti was a master. AT BOTH.

Chapter 13

MAFIA, LLC
The Conti Story Continues

Saturday morning Peter awoke and went downstairs to the breakfast room where Hazel, his cook, had prepared a wonderful meal for him. He grabbed the weekend edition of The Buffalo Evening News that Hazel had already laid out on the table for him. An article in the political section read:

Peter Conti, a well-known businessman in the Greater Buffalo Area has been named to the Board of Directors of our famous Children's Hospital. His appointment to the position will begin immediately. The remainder of the Board members including our Honorable Mayor Stonemetz have stated how proud and happy they are to receive Mr. Conti into their fold, said a spokesperson for the Mayor.

The Mayor's office wanted to inform those of you who are not aware of Peter Conti's impressive Vietnam War record just who this man is. Peter Conti, formally Special Forces' Green Beret Sergeant Peter Conti, is the highest decorated Vietnam combat soldier honored from the State of New York. Along with numerous other medals Peter was awarded the Distinguished Service Cross, our Nation's second highest award for military valor, behind only the Congressional Medal of Honor. The Distinguished Service Cross was established in

1918 to honor heroism. Thank you, Mr. Conti, for your service. You are one of our State's favorite sons.

Mayor Stonemetz was quoted saying, "It is his privilege to serve on the Board with Peter Conti and an honor to be called his friend!"

In more news………..

Peter had a giant smile on his face after reading the favorable article. Yes, he was glad that this article would quiet some of the rumors that were floating around about him, but he was even happier that he was going to be able to help sick and needy children. Remember, when the Russian syndicate gunned down his wife, she was pregnant at the time. Peter lost his wife and child in one horrifying minute. Those who perpetuated the horrific event have already paid with their lives. Not anywhere near enough for Peter, but, if he can help other children it would give him some pleasure knowing he was saving other kid's lives. He was going to pour himself into that quest.

To make a wonderful morning even better, Hazel placed the mail on the table. There right in front of him were the personal invitations to the Mayor's party, every invite, stareing him in the face. His was there, of course, along with one for his parents, his in-laws, and his brother and sister were there too; he couldn't wait to deliver them personally.

The first stop was a difficult one. Peter was going to Jackie's parent's house to deliver their invitations. He hadn't seen them in a very long time. Couldn't face them. It was just too hard for him. But time does heal all wounds, maybe not heal, but it does ease some of the pain. It was time. The meeting with his brother-in-law Tommy was proof of that. So, there he stood at the front door hesitant to ring the bell, but ding dong.

"Oh, my goodness," said a very surprised Patti Millen.

"Hi Patti. How are you?"

She looked dumbfounded for a second, but quickly said, "Fine Peter. How are you? Come in. Come in."

"I can just stay a minute. Is Mike home?"

"Yes. Mike, Mike, come here would you honey."

"Jesus, Peter. How are you doing son?"

Peter hugged his mother-in-law and shook the hand of his father-in-law and said, "I'm doing OK. Probably better than OK in some respects."

Mike added, "I know. I just read a beautiful article in the paper about you. We felt very proud of you son, very proud, always have."

"That's what I'm doing here. The Mayor is having a get together at his home next week, sort of an introduction meeting for me to the uppity ups. He asked if my family would like to attend, so."

Peter handed them the personal invitation that was written out to Michael and Patricia Millen.

"Oh my!" said Mike. "Wow, this is an honor Peter. Thank you. We'd love to go."

"Great. I have one here for Jill and Tom as well. Would you give it to them for me, please? Bottom line you guys, my grief has made me stupid as far as our relationship goes and I apologize for staying away for so so long. Please forgive me."

"Don't be silly," said Patti. "We all understood. Sometimes things happen that are so inconceivable that no one knows how to handle it. There is no blame, only sadness. We have missed you though Peter. And think about you often."

"Can you stay a few minutes son?" asked Mike.

"No. I really have to get going."

"Please, just a cup of coffee. We haven't talked in so long. We just want to hear about you and your family."

"OK, yeah, sure. It is really great to see you both. I missed the family, a lot."

The conversation was pleasant and actually rewarding for Peter. The Millens were up on almost everything that had transpired in Peter's life. Not the unsavory aspects, but much of the rest. They knew about his inheritance and business success due to the ongoing relationship that they had with Peter's mom and dad. They were definitely family to the Conti's and would be forever. Everyone shared in the great loss. It wasn't Peter's to bear alone. Especially to Mike and Patti. Their lives would never be the same.

Peter left with a warm feeling in his heart for his in-laws. Feelings that he's had for decades, but for self-protected reasons he kept buried. He was wrong about that. Jackie's death was not only his cross to bear. They were wonderful people and he loved them. He left their house to go around the corner to his parents with renewed spirits. He was about to hand his mom the invitation to go with him to the Mayor's home for a party in his honor. It doesn't get much better for a parent then that. Their child was now rubbing elbows with the elite of the city and the aristocrats of the state. This was going to be a gala event in which politicians from all over the state would attend. Including a few Senators. Peter was anxious to hand them the invite. It was a good day.

There was one more thing that was running through Peter's head as he left the Millen's home. It was one word that kept running and running through his head; WHY???

Chapter 14

MAFIA, LLC
The Conti Story Continues

The last thing on Peter's mind as he walked into his mom's house was, the Mafia. Yes, he was still The Man, that point was irrefutable, but not right now. Right now, he was a little boy showing his mom and dad how good he was doing, in his other life that is.

Joy was the only word that comes to mind when Theresa Conti read the invitation. No not just joy, joy and pride. Thomas shook his son's hand and then hugged him.

"Quite a proud day for our family son. Quite a proud day," said Tom with a giant smile on his face.

Peter left Russ and Marie's invitations with his folks and headed home. He did mention that it would be nice if they could all meet, including the Millen family, before the event so they could enter the Mayor's house together. Two reasons, one he knew it would make all of them feel more comfortable if they entered with him. Two, he wanted to see the look on all their faces.

The week flew by. Theresa had a mid-afternoon lunch for everyone at her house just so the Conti and Millen children could be reunited. It had been years since they were all together. I say children, but the Conti and Millen offspring were all in their early to late 30's. They weren't kids anymore. They all hugged each other as they entered. Jill and Peter's hug lasted a long while. They both cried. Some sadness never goes away. They both wiped their tears and a sad moment turned into a joyous reunion. Tommy pulled Russ aside and told him of the happenings with Peter and the hood that was trying to extort money from him.

"Peter kicked the shit out the guys in 30 seconds. Man, it was botta boom botta bing and this guy was a bloody mess. Then Peter whispered something to the guy and I'm not sure, but I think the guy pissed his pants. Goddamn Peter is a bad ass," said Tommy matter of factly.

"My brother. The man never ceases to amaze me."

"Don't say anything about this to anyone. I'm pretty sure Peter doesn't want to publicize this. He's a big shot now," Tom said laughing.

"Can you believe this guy? I can't believe were going to the Mayor's mansion to a party for him. I'm telling you. It's all unbelievable to me," said a smiling proud brother.

"I know. But cool as shit, ain't it," added Tommy.

"YES. It's freekin mind blowing. I'll tell you Tommy; the whole thing stems from him meeting the Bansano guy. The guy changed my brother's life. You ought to see Peter's house. Jesus Christ it's a freekin mansion. I'll run you and Jill over there sometime. When you see it, you're gonna shit your pants?"

The Conti group arrived right on time and were greeted at the door by Mayor Stonemetz.

"Hello Peter. And hello Conti family," he said as Peter and his family gathered in the enormous entry foyer.

"Mayor Stonemetz, this is my mother Theresa and my father Thomas, my mother-in-law Patti and her husband Michael, my brother Russell and his wife Colleen, my sister Marie, and, last but not least, my sister-in-law Jill and her husband Tom."

"An absolute pleasure to meet you all. Peter is a great guy and I'm happy to call him my friend. Meeting his family makes me very happy.

Now I can see where he gets his good looks," he said directing that last comment to Theresa."

They all said in unison, "Thank you Mr. Mayor."

"You're all welcome. Come on in. The bar is open and it's right over there. I have people walking around with hors d'oeuvres. Please make yourselves at home. Do you mind if I grab Peter for a few minutes? I want to introduce him to the other Board members before this party gets into full swing. Peter, would you mind coming with me for just a moment?"

"Go ahead everyone. I'll catch up with you in just a bit. I'm about to have my 15 seconds of fame," said Peter smiling.

The Mayor spoke up and said, "Don't listen to him. He's already famous. Go enjoy yourselves. We'll be right back."

Peter and the Mayor walked through a double set of doors leading to the library. Standing there were two distinguished looking gentlemen and two lovely and extremely successful ladies. All of them were smiling.

"Please let me introduce everyone. Peter, this talented woman is Irma Waters, CEO of Hallmark Pharmaceuticals. Here we have Ellen Ryan. Ellen is the president of WFCHO, Women for Children's Health Organization. This big guy is Walter Pipen, President of United Bank and Trust. And last, but not least, Paul Roberts, CEO of Tele Systems. Everyone says hello to Peter Conti, war hero, CEO of Zorde International, and the newest member of our distinguished Board of Directors."

Almost in unison they said, "Welcome aboard."

"Thank you all so much. I have been looking forward to this meeting ever since Bob told me the good news. I hope I can carry on with the same enthusiasm and fervor as you have shown with all your hard work for the children."

"Glad we got that out of the way. I wanted you all to meet personally before we go out there and meet and greet our perspective donors. I'll introduce each one of you. Just do your thing and beg for money. The kids could use it. Peter, if you'd like to say a few words, have at it. Let's go have a little fun."

They went back into the great room where most everyone had gathered and mingled. Peter joined up with his family.

"How'd that go son," asked his father.

"About how I expected Dad. They're very intelligent, high-powered people and I'm honored to be on that Board with them. I'm going to have to prove myself I'm pretty sure, but, all in all, I'm going to enjoy the process. It should be rewarding."

Bob came over to where Peter and his family were gathered with one of his colleagues.

"Excuse me folks. Peter Conti and Peter's family, I would like you all to meet our distinguished Senator, James Tobias."

James Tobias, a four-terms Senator out of New York, stuck out his hand to shake Peter's and said, "This is a pleasure Peter. I did my time over their buddy and I remember when the Po Pete scuttlebutt was flying around. You're a hero my friend. Truly a pleasure."

"You've got to be kidding Senator Tobias. I'll bet by the time you heard that story it was so blown out of proportion it was funny. I met a guy at Fort Bragg when I was stateside and I think he said he heard I wiped out half of all the North Vietnam Army, single handed," Peter said laughing.

"Don't kid a kidder, Peter. I was there. I know what you did."

"Well thank you Senator. Senator may I present my family."

Peter introduced his entire entourage and the Senator shook each and everyone's hand. The Conti and the Millen family members were

133

ecstatic. The room was filled with a Whose Who of some of the most important people in the state. To say his family was impressed would be the understatement of the year.

About an hour into the event Mayor Stonemetz introduced the Board of Directors and each one gave their pitch. It went well. The last to be introduced was Peter Conti.

"How about coming up and saying a few words my friend?" signaled the Mayor.

Peter stood front and center and addressed the group with only a few words,

"Thank you, Bob. What a privilege it is to be invited to serve on the Board of Directors for such a great Hospital as the Children's Hospital here in our great city. I'm honored. I am a man of few words and I learned a long time ago that money speaks louder than words. The Children's Hospital heals sick and needy children in spite of their family's financial position in life. These kids need the support of people like us to help. Donations are essential to keep all the good work alive and the hospital doors open. The doctors, nurses, and the rest of the hard-working staff need our help. I'm going to do my part. Bob, I'd like to start the donation ball rolling. Here is a check for $100,000.00. I hope many of you follow my lead. These kids need your support. Thank you all for coming."

"Holy Mackerel. That's a hell of an introduction Peter. On behalf of the rest of us on the Board and all the children that your donation will help, I thank you. Now are you people going to let Peter carry the load or are you going to join in, in the spirit of giving, and give. Give til it hurts. It's for a great cause. My secretary Mary Marlo is sitting at that big desk over there just waiting for you to drop off your checks. Please give what you can. Every dime counts. Thank you all. Now drink and eat to your hearts content. Enjoy everybody."

"Jesus Christ Peter, $100,000.00?" whispered his father.

"Dad, those were Vito's instructions. He was a very generous man. He wanted me to follow in his footsteps when it came to donating time and money. Children's Hospital was his favorite charity and so now it's mine."

"Yeah, but a hundred grand?"

"Yes Dad. Look, I have the money. OK."

"How much money did that guy leave you anyway?"

"A lot."

The party was a great success as the charity pulled in over a million dollars that evening. Peter was a big hit on many fronts. The family had a wonderful, almost unreal time. He made connections with some very high up people from the Western New York area. He started what seemed to be a friendship with a United States Senator. And was received with respect and admiration by his fellow Board members.

WIN, WIN, WIN.

Chapter 15

MAFIA, LLC
The Conti Story Continues

Peter and his family left the Mayor's gets together and was standing in the parking area next to their cars when Tommy said, "Peter. Speaking for Jill and me, I just want to thank you for one of the most enjoyable evenings of our lives. We would never have guessed we'd be attending any kind of function like this. Especially being hosted by the Mayor, at his home for Christ sakes. Thank you, Peter."

"Yes Peter," said Mike. "Patti and I feel the same way. Wow, fella. You never stop impressing us and you've been doing that since you've been a kid. Thank you."

Peter hugged all four of his in-laws and thanked them for coming. But just before they got into their cars to leave, Tommy added, "Before we leave, I have a very important question. Russ tells us you live in like the Taj Mahal. Is there anyway we could see the place? I know I'm excited about it?"

"Come on over now for some coffee before you go home. My brother exaggerates, but I have to admit, it's a nice place. Mom, Dad, Mike, Pat, Russ, Col, Marie, come on over."

"You kids go. Us old people have had enough excitement for one night," answered Thomas.

"BULL, me and Patti are going. I want to see this place."

"OK Mike. You talked us into it," said Thomas with a sly look on his face. He wanted to go just to see the expressions he knew he would see. Peter's home was magnificent. Thomas is just still hesitant to accept everything.

When the cars pulled up you could almost feel the eyes of the Millen family widen.

"Holy shit Peter!" exclaimed Tommy.

"O M G!" was Patti's comment.

Peter came out with his now patented line, "Anybody want to see inside?"

Jill slapped him on his arm, and everybody laughed.

They entered and you could actually hear the loud inhales from the in-laws.

They were standing in the foyer. All four of the first timers, no everyone, even Peter's family who had been there before, were awestruck. The place was simply magnificent. Just then, Hazel, Peter's housekeeper/cook, came out from her quarters. She heard Peter had guests.

"Can I make something for your guests Mr. Conti? Some coffee maybe?"

"No thank you Hazel. I'll take care of that. But thank you. Go on back and do whatever you were doing."

"It would be no problem at all Sir."

"Hazel go. Enjoy the rest of your evening. And Hazel, these aren't guests. This is my family."

"A pleasure to meet you all and, with that, I will say good night."

"Jesus Peter," said Tommy.

"Don't get your panties in a bunch Tommy. She calls me Peter when no one's around. How am I supposed to take care of a house this size by myself? She's great. Come on, I'll show you guys around."

The tour, the coffee, and the conversation were the perfect ending to a perfect night. Peter didn't have everyone over to show off. He had them over because they were the most important people in his life, his real life. And he just wanted to spend more time with them.

When everyone left, there was a common thought running through each of their minds, an undeniable truth. Peter was a very rich and important man.

Chapter 16

MAFIA, LLC
The Conti Story Continues

Meanwhile, in Moscow, Igor Terisenko, the head of the entire Russian crime syndicate, was having a meeting concerning the events of the takeover the Italians perpetrated on his men in America. It was time. He let sleeping dogs lie for a time, but the time was right to reopen the wounds. Sitting around the conference table were; Yuri Mantanko, Terisenko's right hand man, and a half dozen of Mantanko's key men. They were Alexander Turskin, Vladimir Kanokov, Mikhail Krusky, Ivan Bulgakov, Anton Chekhov, Ivan Gogorevsky, and Leo Bolostoy, who just walked in and got an evil stare from Terisenko. These were some bad men, all killers, and all hand-picked by Mantanko.

"Yuri, do you have a set of Ivan Terski's books? He was a good man for me over there and, you being his main contact, must have something."

"Not everything, but enough."

"Enough for me to send some men back in there and recoup our losses?"

"Yes, but not without a fight. The Italians are in there pretty deep Boss."

"I don't give a fuck about the Italians. They took out our whole crew. They're already dead as far as I'm concerned. I just want to make sure we get the business back."

"They're strong Boss. No way we just send a few guys over there and think we can wipe them out. We're going to need a pretty big crew."

"Let me do the thinking here Yuri. You just do what I tell you to do."

"How do you want me to start?"

"Did Anthony Sotto take over for Vito after we put that son of a bitch in the ground?"

"Maybe Boss."

"Maybe? What the fuck kind of answer is that?"

"There's a guy named Peter Conti who we're pretty sure took over."

"Find out. If this Conti guy is the new "Don", he won't be for long. You two, Gogorevshy and Chekhov, I want you guys to go to New York and scope out whatever you can. I need everything you can get on them sons of bitches and I want this Conti guy put down."

Anton Chekhov and Ivan Gogorevsky, two of Yuri's henchmen, were given the proper forged credentials needed to enter the U.S. and were sent on their way.

The new war was just getting started.

*   *   *

Ivan Gogorevsky and Anton Chekov were staying at the Buffalo Hilton Hotel and had already contacted a number of Ivan Tersky's old customers. They were questioned on who Conti's people were, when they collected and for what, and how much they had to pay. They strong-armed them into answers. As soon as they left, Peter's guys were informed.

Peter walked into his office at the Delaware Grill after a great weekend, to a shitstorm. The Russians were coming back!

"Find out who these guys are and where they're staying," said Peter as he addressed all his men in a meeting that was hastily assembled by Tony Sotto.

"Don't do anything yet. I want to find out what they have planned, who sent them, and how many they're sending. We're going to nip this thing in the bud. Those assholes aren't horning in on our business again and that's a fact."

"Boss, we already have the word out to contact us if those pieces of shit show up at any of our places. But they come and go so fast we can't catch up with them," answered Sotto.

"Who are they saying they are and what are they calling themselves?"

"They're calling themselves the Russian Smart Choice. Our customers are happy with us Boss. They have stopped looking at us like we were extorting money, but instead they really think of us as consultants. This plan of yours is working to a tee. They'll cooperate Boss, for sure."

"Good. Then let's find out where the Russian Smart Asses are staying and have a little talk with them. After that, I think Gagino can finish our conversation.

Everyone laughed at Peter's play on words and at its meaning.

"You guys remember how we put out the feelers, you know, when we wanted to find the fucking prick that killed Vito? We knew he was fresh off the boat from Russia, probably couldn't speak English very well, or not at all, and we knew he would be trying to find information about Vito and us. We'll do the same thing again. Same (MO) modus operandi. We all have friends or family who work the service industry; taxi drivers, hotel people, waiters, waitresses, and airport and train people. Somebody's gonna recognize a couple of guys who speak with a bad Russian accent. Let's find these assholes before they hurt one of our clients. Let's show our customers the true meaning of PROTECTION when we find them. Capisce?"

"You got it Boss," answered Tony Sotto.

Off went his entire crew on a mission, a mission that didn't last very long. In fact, it ended that very same night.

Peter had just gotten to bed that same night when he heard a noise coming from the stairway leading up from his entrance foyer. He had loosened a number of treads on either side of the staircase so they would make noise if stepped on. Smart! Peter slid out of bed, reached for the 45 he kept at his bedside and went on the attack. Defense was not his game. He had a pretty good idea concerning what he heard and who it was. If it were the Russians, he wanted to take at least one of them alive.

Anton Chekov searched the upstairs looking through doorways leading to the bedrooms, looking for Peter's sleeping quarters. Gogorevsky was doing the same. Anton was the lucky one or should I say the unlucky one. He stuck his head into the master bedroom, Peter's room, and that's all he got in, his head. Peter grabbed his head and broke his neck like he was killing a chicken for dinner. He was real quiet, almost like he was back in Nam when he was a Green Beret. Now Peter, knowing there were two assailants, carefully stalked the other guy.

He found Gogorevsky in a matter of seconds and had him unconscious in less than that. Peter then called Tony Sotto.

"Tony, come over to my place and get here fast!"

"What happened Boss?"

"We can stop looking for the Russians. One's laying dead upstairs and I got the other one tied up and ready for questioning. Get over here."

"On my way Boss."

Tony got there quickly, and he wasn't alone. Joe Gagino was with him.

Peter had Ivan Gogorevsky tied up in a chair and had already started asking him a bunch of questions. To no avail, I might add.

"Who sent you here?"

"Fuck you!"

"That's funny. You're seconds away from me cutting your throat and pulling your tongue out of the slice. You know what's that's called? It's called a Mexican necktie. How's that sounding, tough guy?"

"I no telling you shit."

"Talk to him, will you Joe? I need some answers. You want some coffee Tony?"

When they came back from the kitchen, Ivan was barely breathing.

"His boss's name is Igor Terisenko. He's the Boss of the Bosses. He's the number one of the whole shoots and shebang. The guys in Moscow," said a smiling Joe Gagino.

"Did you get this guys name Joe?"

"Yeah, Boss. His name is Ivan Gogorevsky."

"Thank you, Joe. Tony was right about you. You do good work. Good job."

"Ivan, Ivan, Ivan, wake up," Peter said shaking the Russian.

"Hello Ivan. I'm Peter Conti. But you already know that. Here's something you probably didn't know. Why you're still breathing. I'll tell you why. It's so you can go back to Russia and tell your boss that you are not welcome here. And that if we see or hear of any of your people coming back, they won't ever see Mother Russia again. You tell him that too. One more thing, you inform him that I am not very happy that he put a hit out on me. That makes me very angry. If I have to get angry again, he's dead. Now he has his business over there, and I have mine over here. He needs to be happy with that. Tell Terisenko it's a lot better than being dead. And I mean dead, dead, dead. You got all that."

He turned to Tony and said, "Clean him up and send him back to Russia. I want that message delivered. But if he gives you too much trouble, kill him. Oh yeah, one more thing. Grab his partner's body. It's upstairs. I dragged it onto the balcony foyer. Take it with you. Get rid of it. I don't need this shit. I really don't."

Tony and Joe were gone in minutes. They found Anton's body just where Peter said it was. The guy's head was facing backward in the other direction. They picked up his body and, as they left, you could overhear Tony telling Joe, "I told you man, Conti is a bad motherfucker. I mean one bad ass, tough son of a bitch. I wouldn't fuck with him for all the tea in China."

"You don't have to tell me that twice. I got eyes. That reminds me, I got a question that's been bugging me ever since I met the boss Tony."

"Shoot."

"This Flower Man thing?"

"Stop, right there. The Flower Man is gone. Period. Don't mention him again and for sure not in front of Conti. You understand Joe?"

"Enough said."

"Take a good look at this assholes head. I'm surprised it's still attached to his body. I'll say it again. Conti is a bad motherfucker. Now let's get out of here and do what we're told."

"OK. But grab this guy's feet will you Tony. He's heavy. This other jerkoff ain't going anywhere. When we're done, let's get something to eat. OK? I'm hungry."

Chapter 17

Mafia, LLC
The Conti Story Continues

The next morning Peter told Tony to gather the men together, again. He doesn't like to organize the guys as often as he's had to lately because the police are always lurking around when he does. They're always sneaking around trying to find out anything they can. But he had to, this Russian thing was too important not to address.

"You can stop looking for the two Russians. I found them, or shall I say, they found me. One lost his head over the deal and the other was sent packing back to Mother Russia to let his friends know what would happen if they try anything over here again. Listen up guys, with that said, that don't mean shit to these assholes. Keep your people's eyes open for any Russians entering our city. Anybody Russian and I mean anybody. And watch your backs. This isn't over, I can tell you that. They won't give up this easy, for two reasons. One, they lost a lot of money here and they want it back. Two, revenge. They won't be playing games. We won't let them sneak up on us though. If they do come, which they will, they won't be going home, if you get my drift. Eyes and ears open. Capisce?

Peter looked around the room and saw Paul Parisi sitting at one of the tables and continued with,

"Paulie. I got a question for you."

"What's up Boss?"

"You tell me. I hear things you know."

"What did I do Boss?"

"I hear you been talking to somebody in the Gino Carbone Family over in Vegas. Is this true?"

"Yeah, Boss. I talked with Bobby Russo. He's my wife's cousin. We talked about buying some land over in Belize. Did I do something wrong?"

"No Paulie. You didn't do anything wrong, but this goes for every one of you guys and listen closely to what I'm saying here. NO ONE TALKS TO ANYBODY IN ANY OTHER FAMILY ABOUT OUR FAMILY, ESPECIALLY NO NAMES. NOT A WORD OF WHAT WE'RE DOING OR HOW WE'RE DOING IT. NOT A WORD. I hope I made myself clear. We're making money hand over fist with our new strategy here. Let's keep it that way. Does everyone understand what I'm saying?"

"Yes Boss," was said in unison.

"Now go make us some money and keep your ears to the ground and your noses in the air. We got a war brewing again. I'm telling you these fucking Russians aren't through. Be smart. Talk to your spies out there and stay in touch with them.

*   *   *

A few days later in Moscow.

"Who the fuck does this Peter Conti think he's talking to? These fucking Wops got a big surprise coming. Stay out or we're dead? HA! I'll tell you who's going to be dead. That motherfucking Conti, that's who."

"Tell me again what he said, Gogoresky."

Ivan repeated precisely the message Peter wanted delivered.

"And you're saying he killed Anton, but you didn't hear a shot."

"He broke his neck Boss. I saw Anton laying there with his head looking backward. It was ugly."

"Well, we're just going to have to break Conti's fucking neck then too. It's as simple as that. Who do we have that can mutilate this motherfucker?"

"Turskin. Alex Turskin could pull his head right off. He's as strong as an ox and as quiet as a mouse, Boss."

"Send him to me."

An hour later Alexander Turskin walked into Igor Terisenko's office.

"You wanted to see me Boss."

"Yeah, I need you for a job. I want this guy in New York dead. I'm talking six feet under. Not just dead, I want you to disfigure this son of a bitch. He broke Checkov's neck, so I want you do the same thing to him."

"Who Boss?"

"Conti, Peter Conti. He heads up the crew that took out our guys in New York. I want this to be a message back to his people. A big message."

"OK Boss. Get me the paperwork. I just need to go stateside, and it's done."

"Not so fast. I want you to wait awhile before you go. Let them think we're not coming. When they have their guard down, I'll send you in. But first thing when you get there, I want you to get all the intel you can on his people and his operation. Then I want you to kill that prick. When that's done, I'll send a team over there and kill them all."

"Whatever you say. You're the boss. Just get me the information on this Conti guy and count on it. He's as good as dead."

"Not just dead Turski. Mangled."

"Done."

*   *   *

Business was booming for Peter and his men. Peter implemented a scratch my back and I'll scratch yours plan that worked for a good number of their clientele. That's where they were buying products and supplies from each another and each would reciprocate, increasing all their business.

Peter strolled into the Delaware Grill. Tony, Vic Desica, Vito Sordi, and Al Nazzi were all sitting around a table having lunch.

"Hey Boss," said Tony Sotto.

"Hello gentlemen. How's tricks?"

"Glad you asked Godfather," said a smiling Vic Desica. "Jay."

Jay is all he got out of his mouth when Peter said, "STOP. No names."

"Oh yeah. I mean the owner of the White Cab Company told me that that Greenberg guy has left town, left town for good. My guy is so happy he almost kissed me. This from a man who wished I was dead a year ago. This business thing of yours Boss, fantastic, fucking fantastic."

Every guy at the table shook their heads up and down in agreement.

"Good," said Peter.

"What the fuck did you do Boss?" asked Vic.

"Business my friend. Just business. How many times have I told you? Breaking heads will only get you so far. Killing people will get you sent up and put away for a long time. Business, now that's how you maximize earnings."

"That's why you're the Boss, Boss," interjected Tony.

"I got good people. It takes good people to follow a leader without question. That's all of you guys. Believe me, we're still just getting started. Mangia (eat), I got shit I have to take care of in my office."

"Ciao Boss," said Tony.

Peter made a few calls and, while he was in the midst of lining up a few perspective donors for the Hospital, the other line rang.

"Peter Conti?"

"Yes."

"Please hold for the Mayor."

"Peter?"

"Hi Bob."

"Have you eaten lunch yet?"

"Nope, just got in the office."

"Do you have some time?"

"Yeah, sure Bob. What's up?"

"I'm meeting with Jennifer Taylor Grier, our US Ambassador to The Soviet Union. She just happens to be in town on a personal matter and invited me to lunch. I thought since you're single and she is an extremely beautiful single woman you might want to join us."

"Bob, what are you now, Cupid? Thanks for thinking about me. But the bottom line is I'd love to meet you both for lunch, she being good looking or not. Where and when?"

"Well, OK, I'll be honest. I really called because I thought maybe you could walk us in at Antonio's."

"You sly dog. You're wangling a free lunch, aren't you?"

"Not if Antonio's takes food stamps. I'll buy then," he said laughing.

Peter burst out laughing and said, "Food stamps my ass. You got more money than God. What time do you want to meet?"

"Is an hour good?"

"See you there. And Bob, thanks for the invite. I'm serious. I'd love to meet her and not because she's beautiful and single, of course, that doesn't hurt."

"You're welcome buddy. Looking forward to seeing you. And thank you. I'm the friggen Mayor and I can't get a reservation. Who are you anyway?"

"I'm on the Board of Directors of the prestigious Children's Hospital. That's who I am."

"Bull."

"I just feel lucky we're friends and I'll see you there," said Peter.

What a Godsend for Peter and just at the perfect time. The Russian syndicate is knocking at his door and there's a chance Peter might have to take the fight to them. What luck. If he could somehow sweet-talk this Jennifer woman into a date, after all she is a single woman and Bob said pretty. That doesn't hurt. Maybe just maybe, he could start a relationship, one that would be instrumental for his needs.

Question is, is she even available. He had to try. This was too perfect to pass up. She must spend a goodly amount of time in Russia. What better alibi could he have then to go there because he's visiting a lady friend? He hadn't dated any woman other than Jackie since he was 16 years old, but he was quite a handsome and successful man. He did have that going for him. It was worth a try.

All of this was running through Peter's head as he drove to Antonio's. Business, all he could think about was the business aspect of this. He had no interest in dating, but this opportunity was just too good to pass up. He was going to give it his all. He just knew he couldn't come on too fast. He didn't know what to do and he knew it.

"This is stupid," he thought to himself. "What do I have to lose," he continued thinking almost out loud. "I hope Bob wasn't bullshitting me about her being pretty. There's no way I can pull this off if she isn't."

He had almost talked himself out of it when he pulled up to the parking lot. Mayor Stonemetz pulled in at just about the same moment and they parked right next to each other. Peter got out of the car and walked over to open the door for the Ambassador.

When she exited the car, Peter's heart was pounding. He did not expect her to look like she looked. She was breathtakingly beautiful. Peter was speechless for a moment, but was able to eke out, "Excuse me for stareing Miss Ambassador. Bob said you were a lovely woman, but he didn't say you were stunning. It is such a great pleasure to meet you. Peter Conti at your service."

"How do you do Mr. Conti? My name is Jennifer Taylor Grier. The pleasure is mine. Bob hasn't stopped talking about you since we got in the car. Your resume is impressive Sir."

"Bob exaggerates. Yes, I did save all 50 of those babies from that burning building but anybody would have repeatedly jumped back into the roaring flames to do that. Is that what you told her Bob?"

"No Peter. I told her you were in the Army."

151

"Well that too."

All three laughed.

"No, seriously Miss Grier it truly is my pleasure. I hope you're hungry. The food here is absolutely wonderful."

They walked in and Peter got his usual greeting from the owner.

"Mr. Mayor, a pleasure to see you again Sir and hello Peter. Every time you come in you surprise me. This time you come in with the Mayor and I'm assuming Miss America."

Peter laughed out loud, "Antonio Scavazzo this is the US Ambassador to the Soviet Union, Miss Jennifer Taylor Grier."

"A pleasure to serve you Miss and welcome to Antonio's."

"Thank you, Sir. What a wonderful place you have here."

Antonio snapped his fingers and Pasquale Tocco, Antonio's headwaiter, escorted the small group to Peter's private table.

"What can I get your party to drink Mr. Conti?"

"Son of a bitch. I'm the Mayor and he asks you?"

"What can I say Bob. It's all about those 50 babies."

They all laughed again.

"Miss?"

"Vodka Martini with two olives, please."

"Your Honor?"

"Bloody Mary, if you will sir."

"Mr. Conti? Dewers on the rocks with a splash?"

"Yes. Thank you, Pasquale."

"I'll bring your drinks and be back to take your food order when you signal me Mr. Conti."

"That's perfect. Thank you."

With a smile that would knock a buzzard off of a dead cow, the Ambassador said, "Have you ever been here before, Mr. Conti?"

"As a matter of fact, I have. Miss Grier. And is there any chance you could call me Peter?"

"I would be happy too. If you call me Jennifer."

"Wait, what am I a piece of bologna over here?"

"Excuse me Bob, but have you noticed how pretty this woman is? I'm just saying."

"Shut up. I want to talk business," injected the Mayor.

"What business?"

"Jennifer here is from our sister city, Rochester, and is very interested in helping with our Children's Hospital Charity Drive."

"That's right Peter. I was involved before when I was a congresswoman living in Rochester. It's a marvelous cause and I would like to help in any way I can."

"How long will you be in town, may I ask?"

"I'll be here through the weekend. A very close friend of mine is getting married Saturday here at the Cathedral and then a reception over at the Ritz. I'm not leaving until late on Sunday."

"Great. That will give me a few days to put something together. Thank you, Jennifer. Your involvement will certainly help in our fundraising. Let me figure the best way we can put a famous person with your credentials to use. This could be big. We should be able to turn your endorsement into some big money for the kids. Thank again Jennifer. Thank you very much."

Peter turned to Bob and said, "Bob, no wonder you keep getting elected term after term, you are a very smart man."

"That's right Peter I am. You know I have a giant size QI."

"That's IQ Bob."

"Oh yeah."

"Everyone laughed again."

The lunch went perfectly. Just before they were getting ready to leave, Antonio's daughter came over to the table, kissed Peter on the cheek as usual, and as usual told him how grateful she was.

As she walked away the Mayor said, "I never asked you what that was about?"

"Great kid isn't she. I helped her out of a jam a while back and she never has forgotten. It was my pleasure, believe me."

He left it at that and said, "Jennifer, not to be bold, but I'm having a small dinner party at my home this evening. That would be a perfect time for us to discuss some possibilities. If you don't have plans, I would love to have you attend."

"As a matter of fact, I have no plans for the evening. That sounds lovely. I would love to."

"Who's attending," she asked.

"Just, You and Me" he said with a smile.

"You are something else Mr. Conti. Are you serious?"

"Actually. I am. It would be a good time to discuss some strategies, but if you think I'm being forward."

"No, you're right. I accept."

"Bob, would you and Arlene like to join us?"

"I'd love to Peter, but unfortunately we have a previous engagement. You two kids figure something out about the Charity Drive. I have all the confidence in the world in both of you. You're two of my favorite people in the world."

"OK, where are you staying Jennifer?"

"I'm at the Ritz."

"Then I'll send a driver to pick you up. Is 8:00 OK with you?"

"You were right Bob. This guy is something else. 8:00 would be perfect Peter."

Peter called for the check. Antonio came over and said, "Peter, how many times do I have to tell you, there is no check for you my friend. You are always my guest."

"Antonio, I hate that. But thank you."

The two men shook hands and Antonio said his polite goodbyes to Peter's guests. Peter threw two hundred-dollar bills on the table for a tip and they got up to leave.

"Thank you, Peter. You are such an easy touch. You know that?" said the Mayor.

"Bob, anytime my friend. Anytime. Miss Jennifer Taylor Grier, I look forward to seeing you again later. Enjoy the rest of your day."

"Thank you, Mr. Peter Conti. I look forward to it Sir."

Peter walked them to the Mayor's car and opened the door for the lovely lady. She got in and he closed the door. He then got into his car and he was gone.

WIN, WIN.

Chapter 18

MAFIA, LLC
The Conti Story Continues

Peter drove right home to let Hazel know he was having a business/pleasure guest over for dinner. The entire time he was driving he thought about how he could use the Ambassador for entry into Russia. It was perfect. There was only one problem. He really liked her. She was perfect. He felt terrible using her, but it was too perfect to let slip through his hands. He knew he had to keep his feelings out of it. But it was going to be difficult. Plus, he never did question her to see if she was involved with anyone. She could be living with someone for all he knew. He needed a plan. Access to Russia could be instrumental in his cause.

Jennifer arrived at the front door at 8:15. She looked like a movie star. Peter greeted her on the stairs leading to the giant entry doors. Her beauty was memorizing. Peter walked her through the doors into the foyer.

"Very impressive Peter. What a lovely home."

"Thank you. It's way to big for my taste, but it certainly comes in handy when you're entertaining. May I show you around?"

"I'd love to see it."

He gave the nickel tour not the full nine yards. He didn't want to seem like he was showing off. They ended up on the patio outside of the kitchen area just off the pool. The area consisted of an array of lounging pool seating and a couple of patio tables and chairs. One was set up with service for two. Peter served wine but had the makings for a vodka martini on hand. She chose the wine.

"Do you live here alone Peter?" she asked.

"No. Hazel lives here with me."

"Oh, Bob told me you were a widower."

Just then Hazel came out carrying a tray of a variety of hors d'oeuvres.

"Would you care for any hors d'oeuvres Miss?"

"Just put them down on the table Hazel. We'll snack on them a little later. She is plying me with wine right now. She's so obvious."

Hazel just laughed. He always made her laugh.

"Yes Sir," she said still giggling.

"That's Hazel?" she asked.

"Yeah. Isn't she great?"

"You know she calls me Peter when no ones around. Couldn't live here without her."

"Peter, I was kind of referring to a companion when I asked if you lived here alone."

"Oh, no, I live here alone," he said with a sly smile. "I'm unattached. How about you? Someone as beautiful as you must have her pick of the litter."

"My position keeps me too busy for that, although I get hit on every day. It's maddening sometimes."

"Me too," he said almost laughing.

"I bet you do. You're not that disgusting looking."

Just what Peter wanted to hear, joking and familiarity.

"Disgusting looking? Now I can see I wasted my time washing under my arms with a washcloth just cause I knew you were coming."

Jennifer burst out laughing.

Hazel came out and said, "The hot dogs will be ready soon Sir."

She hesitated a moment and then said, "I'm sorry Miss, he made me say that."

Jennifer burst out laughing again.

"We have Cornish game hens or steak or both miss. Which do you prefer?"

"The game hen sounds lovely. Thank you, Hazel."

"You're welcome Miss. And you Sir."

"The bird sounds nice. Thanks Hazel. Oh Hazel, how long before you plan on serving?"

"Up to you Sir. Would an hour suit you?"

"Perfect. One more thing Hazel, would you please bring another bottle of wine out?"

The dinner was perfect. The conversation was light, but interesting. Jennifer talked about her duties in Russia without giving away any trade secrets. Peter just said he had his fingers in a number of businesses and that business was good. After dinner they were having an aperitif, in this case a glass of Sherry, and then some coffee. Then out of the blue Jennifer asked, "Peter, would I be too invasive if I asked you about your time in Vietnam. I'm sorry, but Bob was saying some braggadocios things about you. If I struck a bad chord, please don't answer."

"Gee Jenny, I mean Jennifer."

"Oh, please Jenny is fine."

"Well, I bet he didn't tell you I was scared the entire time I was there."

"No, he told me you were the most decorated soldier to come out of this state when you were over there. He told me you were Special Forces Green Beret."

"Oh yeah. That too, I forgot. Yes, I was that."

She laughed, "Peter, come on, tell me something, I'm interested."

"Jenny. Did you ever hear the expression WAR IS HELL? Well whoever said that was right. You have guys dying all around you and all you can think of is what can I do to stop this. That's what I tried to do. Yes, no denying, I definitely took lives. It's so terrible to even say that it still haunts me. BUT I was teamed up with four other Green Beret soldiers and we made a pretty impressive unit. All I can say is that we saved countless American lives. That's what I'm proud of. Not the medals. I hope that's enough information about that for you."

"It is Peter, thank you. But I have only one smaller question concerning all that. What does Po Jing Pete mean?"

"That answers for another time. How about some dessert? We have hot dogs!"

Jennifer burst out laughing again.

They had a few discussions about the charity business, but the night turned out to be just a pleasant and enjoyable evening of entertainment for both of them.

"We didn't get a chance to talk much about the Hospital Charity Drive. I have been kicking around a few ideas, but it's late. Any chance you have some time tomorrow. I know you must have a busy schedule, but if we could meet maybe for lunch," asked Peter.

"I'm on vacation. I have no schedule. This has been an absolutely wonderful evening and you are a charming man. I would love to see you again tomorrow."

"Does that mean, Yes?"

Then something happened that staggered Peter for a second, bringing back memories of the love of his life. After he said that Jennifer, slapped him on the shoulder, exactly the way and exactly the same spot as Jackie. He hesitated before saying anything and as he found his way back to reality he said, "Owww. Oh my God you broke my arm."

She hit him again. Same spot. Just like Jackie.

I'm not sure if it's been mentioned, but Peter is not only extremely handsome, he's also built like a brick shithouse.

"So that does mean yes," he replied.

"Yes. Is that more clear?"

"Great. How about having lunch over in Canada at Niagara Falls?"

"Are you firing on me Mr. Conti?"

"Noooo. Well, maybe a little. Are you offended?"

"Not in the least. I was just about to fire on you."

This time Peter burst out laughing.

"Come on. I'll take you back to your hotel. What do you think about starting our lunch outing about 9:00 AM?"

"That's a little early for lunch don't you think."

"Well, I was thinking about starting lunch out with a little breakfast. What do you say? Do you have the time?"

"I say, you move very fast Mr. Conti."

"Well?"

"Sounds great."

"I'll ring you up just at 9:00. Try and look a little better than you did tonight."

"Sir. I resent that comment," she said laughing.

"Well maybe you didn't understand what I was saying. What I meant by that is, you can try and look better tomorrow than you do tonight, but I am very aware that that would be nearly impossible because you look absolutely stunning tonight."

"Now there's a line for you."

"Did it work?"

"Maybe."

"Let me take you back before I do something I'll regret."

"What do you mean by that Sir."

"This."

Peter didn't want to take this chance, but it seemed like a good idea at the time. He reached over and kissed her. Not a passionate kiss, but definitely a kiss.

"Well, that was unexpected," she said.

"I know. Why did you do that?" he replied

"What do you mean me?"

"I'm sorry. I couldn't help myself," he said.

"I would have been mad if you didn't."

He took her back to the Ritz and left. Tomorrow was another day.

Chapter 19

MAFIA, LLC
The Conti Story Continues

Peter showed up right on time and buzzed her room. Five minutes later Jennifer walked out of the elevator casually dressed.

"Well I'll be," said Peter.

"What do you mean by that?"

"I really thought that it would be impossible for you to look prettier than you did last night. But I was wrong. You look radiant."

"Are you starting with lines at 9:00 o'clock in the morning?"

"That's not a line. You look great."

"You must be a fantastic salesman, is all I can say."

"Jenny, fact is fact."

"Well then, thank you. You don't look so bad yourself."

"Thanks, I took a shower, too."

She laughed and said, "Would you like to have breakfast right here in the dining room?"

"No. I have a place in mind that I really think you'll like. The atmosphere is very pleasant, and the food is great."

"OK, sounds very nice, let's go."

They headed over to Allen Street, a quaint area in Buffalo that somewhat emulates Greenwich Village in New York, for a light breakfast at one of its open cafes.

They pulled up to Yaya's Bistro and Bakery, were seated at a comfortable table with a very nice view and ordered coffee to start.

Peter was even more torn as he gazed across the table at Jenny. The sun was framing her outline and her face was like an angel's. It didn't matter. He needed this connection. He somehow had to stay focused on the task at hand. But it was getting harder and harder by the minute.

"I love this place Peter. Thank you."

"You are welcome. I knew this would suit you."

"How do you know that? You barely know me."

"Please. You may be complicated when it comes to government work, but I saw the real you last night. Warm, caring, funny, and smart but down to earth. Best way I can explain it is, I see a woman who is complex when she needs to be, but simple when it comes to life. I can tell you are extremely family oriented by the way you talked about your family during our conversations. Plus, you're here because a good friend, a friend who was almost like family, was getting married. US Ambassadors don't do that kind of thing unless they are big time family and friend oriented. Look, I know you are beautiful on the outside, anybody can see that, but what I learned last night about you is that you're even more beautiful on the inside. There, you happy now, you made me embarrass the shit out of myself in less than a half an hour."

"I'm the one who's embarrassed. Wow. You really must be horney!"

"I didn't say that because of that. I said that so that you might pick up the check!"

Jenny laughed so hard she almost spilled her coffee.

The rest of the breakfast was spent laughing and joking and just having a great time. Peter was sweeping her off her feet. This was not working out the way he wanted. You see, Peter was falling for her as well. He needed another plan.

Business. There had to be a way he could combine business with pleasure. But he couldn't think of anything, anything at all. His brain was on hold. All he could do was stare at Jenny. Is it possible he thought to himself? Is it possible to fall in love again? He wasn't sure, but it sure felt like it because everything he's said and done at least to this point had nothing to do with business and everything to do with the woman he was with. She was wonderful in every way.

They hopped back into Peter's two-seater Mercedes and started towards Niagara Falls. Peter decided he could kill two birds with one stone by taking a two-mile detour.

"Jenny, would it be an inconvenience, well not really an inconvenience, more like a horrible chore, if we made a quick stop."

"Now what? I'm not sure I trust you."

"It's my parents. They have been all over me for a long time to date again. I'm too busy for that, but since this is sort of a date, would you mind just saying hello? Just a minute or two, really. It will definitely get them off my back."

"That's not a chore. That would be a pleasure. I would love to meet them."

"Yeah, you say that now."

"No. Really."

"Great, you have no idea how much an Italian mother can nag."

She laughed.

A few minutes later they were parked in his parent's driveway.

"You're sure now."

"Peter, no problem."

"Ok. I warned you."

Peter walked in the kitchen door just ahead of Jenny. His mother and father, along with his brother Russell and sister-in-law Colleen, were sitting at the table having coffee.

"Jesus Christ. Look what the cat dragged in," said Russell.

"Hi everyone. Just dropped in for a minute. We're on our way to the Falls. Everyone, this is Jennifer Grier."

"Hiii," she said.

"Jenny, this is my mom Theresa and dad Thomas. This beautiful woman is my sister-in law and she had the misfortune of marrying my brother Russ."

"It is a pleasure meeting all of you. Peter has spoken very highly of each and every one of you. Sorry Marie isn't here. I would have liked to have met her as well."

Russ spoke first. "Sorry that you're blind Jennifer, but really he's not that terrible a looking guy."

"I think he's handsome."

"Please come in. Sit down. Let me fix you something to eat," said Theresa.

"Oh, thank you but no. We just had breakfast," she answered.

"How about some coffee?" asked Thomas.

Peter answered, "We just stopped in to say hello. We're going to run."

"NO WAY," said Theresa. "We want to meet your lady friend."

"Let's stay for a cup of coffee Peter," injected Jenny.

"You asked for it."

"My God you're pretty," said Colleen.

"Takes one to know one," Jenny responded.

"I like her Peter," said Colleen.

"Are you a model?" asked Thomas.

"DAD!"

"No Mr. Conti, I am the United States Ambassador to the Soviet Union."

The entire group's mouths dropped open and there was a moment of complete silence.

"It's just a job," said Jenny.

"Jesus Mary and Joseph, Peter," said Russell. "How in the world did you talk this beautiful, intelligent, successful, woman into even getting in a car with you."

"I used my charm and good looks AND I bought her breakfast."

"Jennifer not only are you all the things my son Russ just said, you're also brave," said Thomas.

"He's not that bad after you get to know him."

"That's all. I'm not punishing this woman with you people anymore. I'm taking her to the Falls."

"Come back for dinner," pleaded Theresa.

"I'd love to Mrs. Conti, but I have a previous engagement. Maybe next time."

"Not one person said a word to me. Nothing. I feel slighted," said Peter.

"OK, here are some words, go take this lovely woman to the Falls and call your mother more often. She's always saying, why doesn't he call?"

"I'm sorry. You know I love you mom."

"AWE, I love you too Peter."

"She never ever says that to me! Never," said Russell.

"You want some cheese with that whine," answered Peter.

Everybody laughed.

"We're going."

"It was so nice meeting you all," expressed Jenny.

"The pleasure was ours sweetheart," answered Theresa. "Come back anytime."

They walked out to the car. Peter opened the door for Jenny, but just before he got in on the other side, Russ was at the back door calling Peter over.

"One second Jenny."

"What?"

"What? What? What the hell? The U.S. Ambassador to Russia who looks like Miss America, are you kidding me?"

"You jealous bastard. She's great, isn't she?"

"Call me Goddamn it. I want to hear everything."

"I'll call you Bro, but there's nothing to tell you. I just met her yesterday. But I'll call."

Peter got in the car and quickly said, "Now I owe you big time. Your wish is my command."

"OK. I just thought of something."

"Name it."

"How would you like to go to a wedding tomorrow?"

"NO, absolutely NOT. Wait, do you mean with you. Then, yes of course."

"Great, you just became my plus one."

They had a fantastic time at the Falls, in fact, the entire rest of the day, but it was getting late in the afternoon when Jenny said, "Peter, I don't want this day to end but I really do have a previous engagement. It's with a bunch of my girlfriends from the wedding party that I haven't seen for ages. I need to get back to the hotel to get ready."

"Of course. I understand completely. I guess you can fill me in on times and whatnots for tomorrow. If you still want to go with me. I'm just giving you a chance to let yourself off the hook."

"Don't be silly. I can't wait until tomorrow. I think I'm starting to like you Peter Conti. A lot."

"Shucks Mam. You make a feller blush."

She laughed again.

"Let me get to the room and make some calls. I'll call you within the hour and let you know my schedule for tonight and tomorrow."

"Sounds great."

They were on their way back to the Ritz. When they were getting close, a couple of blocks away, Jenny asked Peter to pull over. This time she kissed him and wow what a kiss.

Peter was caught, hook, line, and sinker.

Chapter 20

MAFIA, LLC
The Conti Story Continues

"Gwen, Jenny."

"Where have you been? We all thought we'd see you today."

"Busy. I just called to see what time the girls are getting together tonight, and I need times and places for tomorrow."

"Don't give me that busy answer. What's up?"

"Gwen. I met someone?"

"Shut your mouth. Tell me everything."

"He's so handsome he makes me melt. He's successful, built like pro football player, and smart. He funny and makes me laugh, all the time."

"Stop it, you're going to make me call off my wedding. All of a sudden Joe's not sounding that great."

"Shut up. Joe's perfect for you."

"I know. I guess I really do love the guy. OK, you talked me into it. I'll still marry him tomorrow but tell me more about your guy. Who is he? How did you meet?"

"He's on the Board of Directors of the Children's Hospital and we met at lunch yesterday. Mayor Stonemetz introduced us. We had lunch at a beautiful Italian restaurant. Maybe you've eaten there, Antonio's."

"Yes, on special occasions. The place is always so packed it's near impossible to get reservations."

"Peter has a private table there and they treated him like he was a king. The owner spent time with us and told him to stop asking for checks because Peter will always be his guest. Peter dropped a few hundred on the table anyway, but my jaw dropped when Antonio said that. Then Antonio's daughter came over and kissed Peter on the cheek and thanked him for I don't know what but thanked him just the same. It was unreal."

"Peter who? Who is this guy?"

"A friend of the Mayor's, his name is Peter Conti."

"Peter Conti, I know that name. The war hero guy they've been writing about in the papers?"

"Yes, but he doesn't talk about that. Gwen, he's the one! I'm bringing him to the wedding."

"Holy shit, and you just met him yesterday?"

"Yes, but after lunch he asked if I was available to attend a dinner party, he was throwing at his home to discuss a charity thing for the Children's Hospital. I said that I was free and asked who would be there. He said, just you and me. I had to laugh, but I went. Oh my God, you should see his house and it was a perfect night."

"Did you?"

"Stop it, we just met. BUT I wanted to. Does that tell you anything?"

"You'll meet him tomorrow. Tonight, is for us girls."

"Change of plans. The guys are coming too. About a half dozen couples, Joe and I with Judy and Dan, Frankie Ann and Al, Georgette and Kurt, Karen and Rafael, and you guys if you're not embarrassed of us peon's, Miss Ambassador."

"Where and what time?"

"We're meeting at The Cabaret on Main Street at 8:00."

"Great. I'll be there. I have no idea if Peter is available, but I'll ask."

"I would love to meet him. I am so happy for you Jenny. It's about time."

"We'll see. I know how I feel, but we just met. I have no idea if he feels the same."

"Didn't you say he was smart? And I didn't hear you say he was blind. You're the catch girl."

"Gwen, that's why I love you. You have no problem lying to me."

"SHUT UP. Can't wait to see you."

"Me too. See you later."

Jenny hung up the phone and hesitated for a few minutes before she called Peter. She really wanted him to accompany her tonight, but she didn't want to push. She decided she only had a few more days before she had to head back to Russia, so what the heck.

"Peter, Jenny."

"Who?"

"Jenny Grier, oh stop it."

"Do you know your schedule?" he asked.

"That's why I'm calling. Tonight, my girlfriends and I were getting together, but the plan changed and they're bringing their husbands. I was wondering if you had plans for the evening and, if you didn't, maybe you might want to join me?"

"Sorry Jenny, I'm cleaning my bowling ball tonight."

Jenny laughed out loud right over the phone.

"Great," said Peter. "I'd love to. Where, when, and what do you want me to do?"

"Just pick me up at the hotel around 7:45. Do you know The Cabaret on Main Street? A number of my friends are meeting there at 8:00. This way you'll have a chance to meet Gwen and Joe, the bride and groom, and a bunch of my childhood friends."

"That sounds wonderful AND I get to spend more time with you."

"You're still horney aren't you?" she said giggling."

"No comment," he responded immediately. "I'll buzz your room."

"And Peter, try and look presentable."

"Do I have to shave?"

"You always make me laugh. See you soon."

Peter drove up to the front door of the nightclub called, The Cabaret in his beautiful Mercedes to drop Jenny off before he parked. Gwen, Joe, Georgette, and Kurt were standing there talking when he pulled up. Jenny got out and immediately hugged them all while Peter parked. The group waited for Peter.

"Everybody, this is my date, Peter Conti. Peter this is the bride to be Gwen who I've known since I was a girl. In fact, I've known all these people all my life it seems. This is Joe her almost husband and this is Georgette and her husband Kurt."

"A pleasure meeting you. Thank you, Gwen and Joe, for inviting me," said Peter politely.

"Is that a joke," said Gwen. "When Jenny told us she met someone, we couldn't wait to meet you. You're right Jenny he IS handsome."

Jenny responded with, "He's taken and you're getting married tomorrow."

"Oh Yeah, I forgot for a second. Joe, you're even more handsome honey so don't get jealous."

"Jealous, what are you talking about? I think he's handsome too!"

Everybody laughed and went inside. Peter met the rest of the crew that were already seated, and the night began. It was a terrific night for everyone. Drinking, dancing, laughing, everyone there was having a great time and then the trouble started. A couple of guys who were standing at the bar were staring at Jenny all night. Peter noticed but said and did nothing. He was watching though. Finally, Jenny and Gwen got up to go to the ladie's room and two of the guys walked over to them. They said something rude to the woman and Jenny retorted quite loudly. One of the guys reached for her arm. Peter was there like a cat. He wasn't polite or politically correct at all when he said, "What the fuck do you think you're doing?"

"This ain't none of your business buddy."

"I'm making it my business," said Peter as the other two guys rose from their bar stools.

Peter turned and calmly said to Jenny's friends, "Sit down guys, I got this."

"Who the hell do you think you are?" asked the guy who had reached for Jenny's arm.

"Somebody you really don't want to mess with. So, if I were you, I would apologize to these ladies, pay your bar tab, and leave quietly or you will be leaving in an ambulance."

Joe, Kurt, Dan, and Rafael weren't about to sit this out even though their wives were trying to keep them out of it.

Joe said to Peter, "Conti. We're right behind you."

"Conti? Did you say Conti? Peter Conti," said the loudmouth as all four of the hoods took a few steps back. The leader continued with, "I'm sorry Mr. Conti. We didn't mean anything by this. Nothing at all I swear. We we're just fooling around. We'll be leaving now. Have a nice evening."
They paid their bill and were gone just like that. Joe turned to Peter and asked what everyone in their party wanted to know, "Peter, who the hell are you?"

"I guess they thought I was that Green Beret guy they been writing about in the paper," answered Peter.

"Jesus," said Joe.

Peter addressed the table and said, "Hey everybody it's over. Don't let this little disturbance spoil the night."

Gwen turned to Joe and whispered, "Jenny told me Peter is that guy from the paper."

They had no idea that it wasn't the Green Beret thing that had those hoodlums shitting their pants. They had no idea at all.

Everyone returned to their seats at the table, everyone but Peter and Jenny that is.

"Are you OK honey?" said Peter realizing it was the first time he called her that.

"Just fine Peter. Tarzan to the rescue."

"Don't be silly. Bullies always back down. But excuse me I have to change my underwear. I think I soiled myself."

Jenny laughed again. She laughed hard, but this time it was Jennifer Taylor Grier, the United States Ambassador, who was caught, hook, line and sinker.

When Peter and Jenny sat down at the table, all eyes were on Peter. Joe confronted Peter and told Peter that Gwen just confirmed that he actually was the Green Beret war hero guy they had all read about in the paper.

"Joe, that was a hundred years ago."

"It didn't look that way to us."

"Here's the thing. It's important that you all look nice for tomorrow's celebration. Right? Me, it doesn't matter what I look like, so I confronted those assholes myself. Besides, usually bullies always back down. I took a chance. One more important thing you all need to know, I'm not brave, I'm stupid. That's what really happened. AND, and this is a very big and, I was trying my best to impress a girl."

Jenny spoke up with, "Mission Accomplished."

Everybody laughed but those people knew what they just saw. They were all impressed.
The night ended and everyone said his or her goodbyes. Tomorrow was a big day.

Chapter 21

MAFIA, LLC
The Conti Story Continues

Jenny was definitely smitten, no that's an understatement, she was falling in love. She held onto Peter's arm tight with both hands as they walked to the car. She was already dreading the fact that she was leaving and going back to Washington D.C. on Sunday, from there on to Russia. She didn't want to leave. Peter drove her back to her hotel. She gave him a passionate kiss in the car and said,

"Stay with me tonight Peter."

Peter hesitated a moment. He shook his head as to say, I don't know what to do, and said, "I want to more than anything in this world Jenny, but I can't."

"Why?"

"There are things that are said about me that could hinder your position as an Ambassador and I don't want you to take that chance."

"What things? I don't understand."

"When Bob told you about me, did he explain how I obtained a big portion of my wealth?"

"No. Not really. He just said you were a hell of a businessman."

"He's right about that, I am. I do well. But my house and a number of my investments came from a very wealth man. A man who semi-adopted me and when he died, he left me many things."

"I don't care about that Peter. I just want to be with you."

"Yes, I understand Jenny, I want to be with you too. But let me finish. Bob was very good friends with this man, and they shared the same passions for helping the sick and the needy. When he died, he left instructions for me to follow. He wanted me to follow in his footsteps, and I am."

"I don't understand what this has to do with anything."

"This man's name was Vito Bansano. Jenny, he left me more than just his house, his reputation went with it as well."

"What are you talking about? What do you mean reputation?"

"His reputation is why it's so important we have this conversation. It was rumored that he had his fingers in racketeering. That he was a gangster. Now because he left me things in his will, of which I'm still completely surprised he did, people are equating me with him. Jenny, I won't take the chance the reputation that's rubbing off on me could rub off on you. I can't allow that. It could ruin your life. Listen sweetheart, I'm not Vito Bansano, I'm Peter Conti. My reputation is held in high acclaim. I think you know that, I guess because of the war hero thing. I hope people look at me as the guy who is heavily involved in our community in many charitable ways. Most importantly, the giving of my time and money is a giant effort to build the Children's Hospital to be one of the biggest and finest hospitals for children in the world. That's the reputation I want. Honey, I haven't had anybody accuse me of a single thing. I swear, I'm Peter Conti not Vito Bansano. The thing that stinks about it all is Vito was a good man. That being said, I'm worried that any affiliation with me could be bad for you. That would break my heart. That's why I won't go up with you. Someone might recognize me. As much as it is something, I want to do more than anything else in the world, I can't let you take that chance. Do you understand?"

"Yes. Peter, I understand. I can't believe I'm saying this, but you leave me no choice. There is only one thing that I can do."

"Don't say it. You are going to break my heart if you do."

"Let's go to your place. I don't need to go into the hotel. I'm sure you have something I can sleep in."

Peter just smiled and said, "I think I can find something."

Jenny came out of the master bathroom adorned in one of Peter's tee shirts and nothing else. Peter's heart dropped. She was radiant. He walked over to her and when they kissed you could almost feel the sparks going off. It was magical.

They walked over to his bed and a night of utter passion began.

It was going to change everything in Peter's mind and in his life forever. He just didn't know how.

They woke up early. Well to be honest they barely slept. They got cleaned up and went down for coffee. Peter's mind was in a quandary. His grand scheme to use this woman for entry into Russia and as an alibi was completely kaput. There was no way no how he would or could follow up on that line of thinking and for good reason. He was head over heals in love with her. But how could this work between them. She's a United States Ambassador and he's a, well he doesn't know what the hell he is anymore. Last night changed him. He needed another plan.

He stared across the table at her without saying a word. She was doing the same. Both of their minds were spinning. Hers because she was leaving the next day and the thought of leaving him was killing her, his because he's The Godfather of a crime family, for Christ sakes, and all of a sudden, he doesn't want to be. What a dilemma.

She broke the silence, "Peter, I want to say something."

"Jenny, we've only known each other three days."

"How do you know what I'm going to say?"

"Because I want to say the same thing and I can't believe it. I don't know what to do."

"What are we going to do? I don't want to leave."

"We're going to enjoy the time we have together for the rest of today and tomorrow until your plane leaves and then we're going to figure something out."

"I don't want to go."

He reached across the table, held her hand, looked into her eyes, and said; "I don't want you to go either, but Jenny you are an important person in this world with an obligation to this Country. There's no way you can stay."

"I'll quit."

"Next year is an election year. President Fowler has served his two terms. There will be a new person in charge. Honey, it's only a year."

"But I love you Peter."

"There, you went and said it."

"Don't you dare."

He stopped her in mid sentence by putting his fingers to her lips and said, "I love you too. We will work this out. Jenny, you know I'm a widower. That's all you know. What you may not know is that I loved my wife with every fiber of my being. I never thought in a million years I could ever feel that way again. But then I met you. We will work this out. But not today, today we are going to a wedding."

"You are a smart man Peter Conti."

"In the immortal words of Mayor Stonemetz, *that's because I have a giant QI.*"

Jenny just laughed.

"Sweetheart the wedding doesn't start until 5:00, what do you want to do until then?" He hesitated for a second and with a giant smile said, "Besides that."

"You decide. I just want to be with you."

"Well, my entire world has changed in the last 24 hours, maybe 48 hours, wait it's really only 44 hours."

"Do you have a point here?" she said flashing that smile of hers that could melt butter.

"Well, my mother did say come back soon and I would like you to meet my parents under different circumstance then yesterday's. Let me put it this way, our relationship has changed since then. I could invite them over for breakfast."

"That would be very nice. But why don't we go there? I'll bet they would be much more comfortable."

"I'll call."

An hour later they were walking into Peter's childhood home again. Guess who was there waiting to meet her? Yup, Peter's sister Marie. Russ and Colleen were there too, of course. Jenny IS an Ambassador of the United States and was coming over for breakfast. That's not an everyday occurrence in the Conti family so all hands were on deck. But that wasn't the real reason they were together. The family was thrilled that Peter was bringing a woman over for the second day in a row. They all knew what that meant and, to be honest, they thought that would never happen again.

Jenny spoke first, "Hi everyone. I hope we're not imposing?" said a smiling Jenny. "And hello to you, you must be Marie. What a pleasure to meet you."

"Yes, I am and hello Jennifer Taylor Grier, United States Ambassador to the Soviet Union."

"Its just Jenny."

"Hi Jenny, the pleasure is all mine. Everyone said you were pretty, but they were wrong, you're gorgeous."

"That's enough sis, I already got the job," joked Peter.

"Sit down honey, coffee?" asked Peter's mom.

"Thank you, Mrs. Conti, that sounds wonderful," answered Jenny.

Just then there was a knock on the back door and Sonny and Rosey walked in.
"Peter, what a surprise, we didn't know you would be here."

"Bullshit. Who called you?"

"What we can't just drop by. Well now that you mention it, Russ may have called. I'm just saying." He turned to Jenny and continued with, "Hi I'm Sonny, Peter's best friend in the entire world and this is my lovely wife Rose, a pleasure to meet you," Sonny said as he kissed Jenny's hand.

"Jesus Christ get out of here Sonny. You're embarrassing me," said Peter.

"Hi Sonny, Rose, I'm Jenny and the pleasure is all mine."

Sonny added and was slapped in the arm by Rosey the moment he said it, "Holy crap you're pretty."

"That's all, leave this house now!" said Peter.

"Your mom said we could stay for breakfast, so there."

Everybody laughed. Even Peter.

They had a lovely breakfast. Everyone was interested and asked Jenny a bunch of questions about her position and about Russia and what not and Jenny reciprocated by asking them questions about their jobs and about kids and stuff. You know normal chitchat. They also asked her how long she would be in town. It was pleasant.

"Unfortunately, I'm leaving tomorrow for Washington D.C. and then on to Moscow."

"Oh, first to Washington D.C. and then on to Russia, I guess you have to meet with the President first," joked Russell.

"Why, yes, as a matter of fact."

"Jesus Peter, who are you? You're definitely not the brother I've known all my life?"

"Russell, it's my charm. What can I tell you?"

Everyone laughed again.

Peter and Jenny said their goodbyes, and left to go back to Peter's to relax, before the wedding that afternoon. Every person in the kitchen was thrilled. Yes, Jenny was everything a man could ever dream of, but that's not the reason they were so happy. It was because Peter was moving on with his life. Jackie would never be forgotten, but Jenny was truly welcome in their world.

Chapter 22

MAFIA, LLC
The Conti Story Continues

They stopped by the hotel so Jenny could get her clothes. She decided to check out knowing she wouldn't be returning to the room that night. Plus, she wanted to spend the remaining time that tonight and next day until her flight with Peter.

Jenny looked so beautiful when she descended the staircase from the upstairs balcony at Peter's that Peter nearly had to catch his breath.

"Jennifer Grier you are a vision of grandeur. You look absolutely beautiful," complimented Peter.

"Thank you, kind sir. I should, I paid a fortune for this dress."

"The only place that dress could possibly look better is if it's crumpled up in a ball next to my bed tonight."

Jenny laughed so hard she snorted. Peter burst out laughing at that.

"No kidding, you look gorgeous."

"Thank you, Peter. I feel pretty in this."

"You'd look pretty in a burlap sack, but all I can say is wow."

"You can stop now. Your chances of getting lucky tonight are already off the chart. Believe me. You look extremely handsome yourself.'

Hazel came out with a camera and took their picture like they were going to the prom.

Peter said, "Take a couple more Hazel and definitely take some of Jennifer for me to frame."

"Hazel will you take one or two of Peter for me."

"Of course, Mam."

It was a few minutes past 4:00 so they headed over to the Cathedral. The wedding was starting at 5:00.

The ceremony went off perfectly. Gwen looked beautiful and Joe had a perpetual smile through the whole thing. It ended, pictures were taken, and everyone headed to the reception.

What a party. Jenny was inundated with friends and some family. She lost her parents in a tragic accident, when she was in college. These are the times she misses them the most. Peter instinctively noticed and, when he found out the reason, she was feeling a little down, he comforted her the best he could. But something like that never goes away.

Al, Kurt, Joe's brother Steve, and Joe were standing toasting with a couple of other people when they spotted Peter standing alone and called him over. Jenny was busy with a montage of people crowding around her. She is famous you know.

"Joe introduced Peter to his brother and friends. "Steve, Bob, Timmy, this is the guy. Peter Conti."

"Nice to meet you Peter. You certainly made an impression on my brother, that's for sure," said Steve.

"Shit happens, you know what I mean Steve. It wasn't a big deal."

"Bullshit," said Kurt. Peter was on those guys like stink on shit and they backed down like they were facing John Wayne in the movie Green Beret."

"Because they were," said Joe.

"Stop it. I can't even touch my toes anymore."

"Yeah sure, bull."

"To change the subject, congratulation Joe. Even though I just met Gwen, I can tell what a sweetheart she is and boy she looks beautiful today, congratulations."

"Thanks buddy. It doesn't look like you're doing to bad yourself."

Kurt injected, "Peter, Jenny was and still is the prettiest girl that ever came out of our school, period."

"Really, I haven't noticed."

Kurt said, "Now who's bullshitting who."

Everyone laughed.

The girls were giving it to Jenny just as bad.

"Jenny, you are too much girl. We're all jealous of you as it is with you working with the President and all the D.C. cocktail parties and everything else. I'm not kidding, I really didn't think I could get any more jealous, BUT THEN, you come in here with that hunk," said Judy.

"He is nice looking isn't he," she replied.

"Nice looking! I'd crawl over a mile of crushed glass just to see him take his shirt off," joked Frankie Ann.

The girls all laughed and laughed, but she probably wasn't kidding. Peter Conti is one handsome man.

The party was breaking up and, even though Jenny was having a wonderful time, she wanted to leave. She knew this was the last night she would be with Peter and she was anxious to spend some alone time with him. Naked.

They left and it turned out Peter was right. That beautiful dress did end up bunched up in a ball next to the bed.

They barely slept again for more reasons then one. The other reason was that there was a lot of talking going on too.

"What are the chances you can visit me when I'm in Washington. I do spend a goodly amount of time in D.C.?"

"What did I tell you about the rumors and innuendo that sometimes surround me. I just don't want to put you in a compromising position."

"I don't care."

"I do, Jenny. You are a very important person."

"Right now, the only important person in the world to me is you."

"If I can squelch some of the rumors, maybe. That's all I can say."

"Maybe isn't good enough. What about coming to Russia. I have a lovely place in St Petersburg, and I can get time off over there. I kind of make my own schedule."

"That sounds great. I think that's doable."

Just exactly what Peter wanted when this whole thing started and now there was no way he would go there with any other intension except to see her.

"I'll only be in D.C. 10 days then I'm off to Russia. Meet me there."

"Hold your horses. I have a number of businesses to run here. I can't just go gallivanting off to the Soviet Union on the drop of a hat."

"Then when?"

"Let's catch our breath."

"The only thing I want to catch is," she said as she reached under the covers."

"Will you stop? It's not a toy," said Peter as he rolled over and kissed her like he was going off to war.

They stayed in bed late the next morning and rose to a beautiful breakfast prepared by Hazel. Jenny got up to get another carafe of coffee. As soon as she got up, Hazel said, "Mam please just call, I'm happy to bring more coffee."

"No need Hazel. I can get it."

Hazel filled the carafe and handed it to Jenny and as she did, she said, "I've never seen him this happy Mam. Never."

Jenny just smiled.

The parting at the airport was a bit somber. There were tears. And Jenny cried too. That's how Peter described it to his family when he saw them next.

But the truth is the kiss as they parted was long and deep and neither of them cared who was watching. They were both saddened as she grabbed her briefcase to go to the gate.

"This isn't goodbye sweetheart. We'll be seeing each other soon. I don't know when or where, but it will be soon."

Just before she left, she whispered in his ear, "I love you."

Peter, in his usual way, whispered back, "Ditto."

She laughed one more time and turned to walk away. Peter reached out and grabbed her hand and kissed her again and said, "I love you too."

Peter turned to walk away. He was a different man than he was less than a week ago, but he wasn't sure he could do anything about it.

Chapter 23

MAFIA, LLC
The Conti Story Continues

The next morning Peter went to the office at the Delaware Grill with a heavy heart. He didn't really want to be there. He wanted to be in Washington D.C.

Tony Sotto walked into Peter's office and said, "Morning Boss, any orders for today?"

"Tony you run this organization. I'm just an idea man."

"Bullshit. You're not just an idea man Peter, you are The Man."

"I have the title, but don't kid yourself, you run things here."

"Thanks for the vote of confidence Boss," said Tony as he walked out of the office.

Just then Peter's phone rang. It was Sofia Bansano, "Hello Peter," she said in broken English.

"What's the matter, what happened?" he asked concernedly.

"Paolo, Gino's best friend of 25 years died yesterday, and Gino is beside himself," she said half in Italian.

"What can I do?"

"Maybe call Gino and talk with him. He is very, how you say, sconvolto (distraught)."

"Of course. It's late there. I'll take care of it in the morning. Sofia, I'm glad you called. I'll try to help all I can. You know how I feel about Gino."

"Grazie Peter, grazie."

Peter called Tony back into his office.

"Tony something has come up and I need to be gone for awhile, something in Italy. This is exactly what we were just talking about. You run things when I'm gone. Matter of fact, I'm making a change right here and now. I'm grabbing my stuff and moving out of this office. I've got a beautiful office in my home and I think I want to work out of there. If you need me, just call me, but you won't. I'll still address the guys here for meetings, but you take care of the everyday bologna. You know more about the goings on then me. Welcome to your new office. This one is yours."

"You sure Boss?"

"Positive. I got a lot of other things I need to address and working out of here interferes with them anyway."

"Whatever you say Boss."

"I'll give you a number that you can get in touch with me if you need me while I'm over there, but I know you can handle anything that's thrown at you. You OK with this?"

"I got this. You sure about the office."

"It's yours. Now I'm out of here. I need to get to Italy, veloce (fast)."

Peter ran home to pack. A phone call wasn't going to be good enough. He was off to Sorrento to be with his newfound family and he needed to comfort his Italian Uncle.

"Dio Mio (Oh my God)," said Sofia as she opened the front door.

"How is he? I came as soon as you called."

"Gino Gino, vieni qui, volce (come here, fast).

Gino turned the corner into the front entrance foyer of their beautiful home with a saddened look on his face and the look turned to joy in an instant.

"Peter, Dio Mio, what are you doing here?"

"Hello Uncle Gino. I heard you had a great loss and I wanted to be here with you. How can I help?"

"Already you have helped me nephew. My friend Paolo, you met him at the restaurant, has died. My heart is sad."

"That's why I'm here. To help you with your sadness."

"My brother was so right about you. I am very glad to see you Peter. What I say to you now is very important. Do not even think of staying anywhere but in our home. Please!"

"I wouldn't think of staying anywhere else."

"Benvenuto. Come in."

Sofia made coffee and the three of them sat and just talked.

"What happened?"

Gino held back the tears when he spoke, "We were just talking on the patio of the restaurant and all of a sudden he just dropped. Heart attack. I did all I could, but by the time help came, he was gone. He was my best friend in life. My heart is broken."

Peter put his hand on Gino's shoulder and said, "Sometimes life just isn't fair." He continued with, "Does Paolo have much family here. You know, to take care of things?"

"Si," said Sofia. Paolo has a big family."

"Have they made arrangements?" he asked Sofia. Gino was just too emotional to ask him questions without breaking into tears. Italian people are extremely emotional, especially with things of this nature.

"All we know is that the wake is tonight and tomorrow, and the funeral is Thursday."

"Has his family contacted you to ask about the possibility of having the breakfast at Bella Vista?"

"No, but I'm sure they know Gino would have it no other way."

"Let's contact them. Who would be the best person to talk to?"

"Paolo's youngest son Gino would make the most sense. He still lives home and can talk things over with his mother Camilla. The poor woman."

"Uncle Gino, let me handle a few things for you. I'll contact Paolo's son Gino and offer the restaurant to their family for the breakfast after the funeral. I'll take care of any cost. Is that ok with you?"

"Thank you, Peter. It is hard for me to talk with Camilla right now. Grazi mille grazi, that would help. But the cost is mine. I need it to be."

"Capisce, Uncle Gino. I will go now."

"Peter," said Sofia. "Angelina and young Gino are good friends. I'm sure she would go with you if you like."

"Grazie Sofia that would make it more comfortable for Paolo's family. Is Angelina around?"

"I will call her. She will be here milli veloce."

Angelina was there within the hour. It was a pleasant reunion for Peter. Angelina is a beautiful woman and Peter had mentioned that to her numerous times when he was there before. He also mentioned numerous times their age difference so Angelina wouldn't get the wrong idea. As far as both of them were concerned, they were cousins.

They went to the Verde's home together and knocked on the door. A red-eyed Camilla Verde answered the door. Angelina hugged her and held on as she broke down again. Angelina introduced Peter as Vito's son from America. Camilla knew who he was.

Peter and Angelina explained how they didn't think it would be necessary to offer the restaurant for the funeral breakfast; of course, it would be there, but, only as a formality, they were there to find out if the family wanted anything special there.

"I don't know these things," was Camilla's answer. "My son Gino is here, maybe you could talk to him?"

"Of course," said Peter.

"Can I get you something to eat Peter, or some coffee?" asked Camilla.

Angelina answered, "Coffee would be nice." She said that hoping it would take Camilla's mind off of the conversation that was about to go down.

After being introduced to Gino who already knew of Peter from his father, the four of them sat around the kitchen table and Peter offered a few suggestions.

"In America, when a great person passes away, the family brings many happy photos to share with all his friends. It's a celebration of a wonderful life. Yes, the sadness is still there, but it is good to realize what he has brought into this world and the happiness he brought. Would you like to do that Gino?"

Gino got up and hugged Peter and with tears in his eyes said, "Thank you my friend, this idea makes my heart feel better. It will help my whole familia. Grazie, milli grazie."

The breakfast was taken care of. Peter and Angelina went back to the Bansano home. Now it was time to spend some quality time with Big Gino.

"Uncle Gino, any chance we can take the boat out? The last time I was here you showed me the Amalfi Coast from the water, and it was breathtaking. Would you mind?"

"I would love to Peter. Good idea. Sofia, Angelina, you want to go on the boat?"

"Yes of course Gino, whatever you want honey," answered Sofia.

"Yes Papa. Can Alberto go with us?"

"Yes, my daughter, your boyfriend is like family. Call him, but we are leaving soon."

"Peter do you mind?" asked Angelina.

"Of course not. I am anxious to meet him."

The boat trip did exactly what Peter wanted it to do. It took Gino's mind off of Paolo and brightened his spirits.

Peter gazed at the majestie of the Amalfi Coastline and the homes and villas that climbed the mountain-like terrain all along it. Every home had such a magnificent view.

It wasn't hard for Peter to look on the Bansano family as his own. Mostly because Gino looked so much like Vito. Peter was perfectly comfortable with them all. To him he was with Vito.

"Uncle Gino, are these homes expensive?"

"Why? Are you thinking of buying? Because, if you are, that would make me very happy, so happy I will pay."

"Peter laughed and said, "If I were to buy one, it would be your brother that buys it for me. I must admit. It is a possibility."

"Well, to be honest, that's where the money would have come from anyway," said Gino.

Peter just laughed.

The funeral was sad but the celebration of Paolo's life at the breakfast was heartwarming to the family and all who attended.

Peter was going to leave right after the ordeal was finished but decided to stay around for a little while longer. He wanted to check things out and gather more information on the possibility of buying a place. He found the perfect one. Having a vacation home on the Amalfi Coast sounded pretty damn good to him. After all, it was now completely obvious; without doubt the Bansano family was a second family to him.

Win, win.

Chapter 24

MAFIA, LLC
The Conti Story Continues

Peter arrived back on American soil with all kinds of thoughts running through his head. In his mind, he justified being the Flower Man because he only killed those who deserved killing. He had no qualms about that. Yes, he had taken lives; too many to mention in the war. Then, revenge for his wife, and that was to the fullest, and finally self-preservation. Because of all that, Peter has found himself in a place he never thought he'd be. Now he's trying to figure a way out. But once you're in, it's near impossible to get out. It was a dilemma. But he wanted out, things have changed, he was in love again. The question what could he do about it kept running over and over in his head. For now, moving out of the Delaware Grill was a start. He left the airport and headed over to meet with Sotto. He needed to check in and find out what went on while he was gone.

"Same old same old Boss. Making money and enjoying it," answered Tony.

"Good. Very good."

"Did you take care of the business you had over there?"

"I did what I could do. Nothing earth shattering. Since you've got things running smoothly, I'm going to work on some charity stuff that I've been trying to get done. I'll be gone for a while. You're still in charge. Hold down the fort."

"Will do Boss."

Peter left the Delaware Grill and headed to City Hall in hopes that he could catch up with the Mayor. Maybe even have lunch. It was worth a try. He had an idea.

Peter called Bob's office in hopes that Bob was free, maybe for lunch. The Mayor didn't have time, but he changed his plans once Peter mentioned he had an idea about making some money for the Hospital. Bob changed his plans for two reasons, one, this Hospital was near and dear to his heart and two, he truly liked Peter. They met at Antonio's.

"I know you met me here just for a free lunch, don't try and kid a kidder, and I sincerely think what you're doing is unbecoming of a man in your position."

"Hasn't anybody ever told you there is no such thing as a free lunch? BUT this is pretty damn close," joked the Mayor.

"Good to see you Bob. How you doing?"

"I'm well my friend. How about you?"

"I couln't be better and it's all because of you. I owe you BIG TIME!"

"What did I do now?"

"Jennifer Taylor Grier. That's what. What a woman and I mean on so many different levels."

"I take it you two hit it off," he said with a giant smile.

"Hit it off. If she would have stayed an extra week, I would have married the woman. And I'm not kidding. Thank you, my friend."

"Congratulations Peter. I had a feeling about you two. Really. She's as beautiful and smart as they come and, since you're completely the opposite, well you know what they say, opposites attract," he said smiling even bigger. In fact, this time he even laughed.

"I would be so mad at you, if that wasn't so true," Peter laughed too.

"No really. You guys are two of my favorite people in this world. Both unattached and both, I won't say lonely, but without that special someone. It was inevitable that you would find each other once you started working together. I just sped up the inevitable."

"Bob, I'm flat hooked. Thank you. Really, thank you."

"Happy for you Peter, tell me more about her. I know her pretty much on a business level only, but she seems so lovely and intelligent."

"She is that and more. She's smart, honest, caring, sexy as hell, loving, everything a man could hope for in a woman. She's perfect."

"So, you're saying you like her then. Well, that should be good for at least three more lunches, wouldn't you say?"

"Lunches, I'll buy you a Goddamn restaurant."

Both men laughed and laughed.

"What I'm really saying is, thank you Bob. Sincerely."

"You're welcome my friend."

"Now what did you guys come up with for the Charity?"

"Nothing Bob. Absolutely and unequivocally nothing."

"Well for Christ's sake. Me Me Me Me Me. Is that all you thought about?"

"Yup. But I do have a pretty good idea for us to take advantage of Jennifer's position though."

"Spit it out pal."

"I was thinking, at this next charity auction that's coming up we could offer a long weekend, say a four day weekend trip for two, airfare and hotels included, you know all inclusive, in Washington D.C. Including a guided tour led by the United States Ambassador to The Soviet Union. The trip would include a personal tour of, the Pentagon, the White House, and the Smithsonian Museum, first class accommodations, and an array of dining experiences. I figured the cost should be around $1500 per person and I'll bet we can get $10,000 to $25,000 per couple for it. Let's say anywhere from 10 to 20 couples, you know a tour bus full. We'll net well over a hundred grand for the Hospital and that would be from just this one auction item. It just adds to our projected goal buddy. Don't you think? I'll even sacrifice myself and go with them. Of course, that is if Jenny agrees to it. What do you think?"

"And you said nothing, absolutely nothing," answered Bob.

"Well? To be honest we didn't talk about the charity much," replied Peter.

"Great idea, wonderful suggestion, have you spoken to Jennifer about it. That could be the big obstacle. I think your right though we should get that kind of money for a trip like that. It's a beautiful vacation and the whole damn thing is a write-off for these people and their companies."

"I'll make the same sacrifice that you're making, if Arlene wants to go."

"Are you insinuating that I am trying to mix business with pleasure?"

"No Peter, I'm not insinuating that, I know you are. I'm just jumping on the bandwagon. The thing about that is we would most definitely have to pay our own way. We can't use proceeds from the auction to pay our way."

"Of course, not Bob. I'll even start the bidding off at say $5,000. You can bid too. We'll get it up there. It's all for charity and, like you say, it is a total write-off. With all the other auction items, we could make a killing for the kids. What do you say?"

"I say I made the right decision when I brought you on board. That's what I say. Why don't you run all of this by Jennifer? I don't know what restrictions the Government has for things like this with people in her position. If she can get it approved, we're in like Flynn."

"I just might have to get on a plane to D.C. to talk to her in person in favor of a phone conversation for something as important as this."

"You dog you."

"The beauty of that Bob, that trip is a write-off too. I love our country!"

Both men laughed.

Peter was on the phone to Jenny that afternoon.

"Jenny, Peter Conti from Buffalo. Do you remember me from about a week ago?"

"Are you that short, fat, bald guy with the missing tooth in front?"

"No, I'm that extremely handsome man that looks like a cross between Paul Newman and Robert Redford."

They both laughed.

"Hi. I'm so happy you called. I've been thinking about you almost nonstop," said Jenny.

"Me too. I'm missing the hell out of you and you just left."

"I hope you're calling to tell me you're coming to see me before I leave for Russia."

"No. I'm calling to tell you I'm coming to see you before you leave for Russia."

"That's what I said!"

"Oh, that's where I heard it."

They both laughed again.

"Are you really coming? I am so happy. I miss you so much Peter. And don't say ditto."

"Not this time. I can't even sleep thinking about you."

"When can you come?"

"When are you scheduled to leave for Russia?"

"Not for 10 days."

"Are you loaded with meetings till then?"

"Yes and no. I'm free over the weekend."

"Then I'll come in on Friday. I don't want to stay at your apartment though. We had that talk. Where's a nice hotel that's not in the center of things?"

"Let's get a room in Baltimore, the Marriott's nice. It's less than an hour away on the Beltline and the Inner Harbor is fantastic."

"I'll book it right now. In fact, I'll have the Mayor's office book it in the Charities name, that way it won't be in mine. I'm still skeptical. By the way, we do have a little charity business to discuss."

"What business?"

"If I tell you, I won't be able to write-off the trip. But you are definitely involved."

"Don't you dare tease me."

"Well, can you get a few weekdays and a weekend off when you're Stateside?"

"Yes, why?"

"Trying to put an auction item together for the Hospital, but we'll talk about it Friday."

"I can't wait. I miss you."

"Me too. Will you wear that same outfit you had on just before we left the bedroom to go down for coffee the other day?"

"Peter, I was naked."

"Right."

"I love you."

"Ditto."

Chapter 25

MAFIA, LLC
The Conti Story Continues

Peter landed at BWI, Baltimore/Washington International Airport, early afternoon Friday. He gave Jenny his itinerary and told her he would check into the Marriott and he would be waiting for her in the bar. He was delighted when he saw her waiting for him at the gate.

The kiss was warm, and the hug was long, neither one cared who was watching. They held hands as they walked to where she had parked her car and off they went. They checked in at the hotel and went up to the room. They were there for hours before they went down to the bar for drinks.

"I don't want you to go."

"I just got here."

"I wanted to start the mantra early."

Peter just laughed, "Do you have a favorite restaurant here Jen?"

"Do you like seafood?"

"Love it."

"I know just the place."

They went across the park to the actual Inner Harbor, a historic seaport and probably the best landmark the City of Baltimore has to offer. It is has been noted as the foremost post-industrial waterfront redevelopment in the world. What they did in that City was amazing. It was renovated in the 1980's and houses Camden Yards, the baseball home of the Baltimore Orioles and Baltimore's famous Inner Harbor Aquarium.
It's only a baseball throw away from an area in the City known as Pigtown. Pigtown's most notable attribute, that's where Babe Ruth himself was born.

Not far from Camden Yard was a restaurant famous for its' seafood called The Surf and Turf. Peter and Jenny didn't have a reservation, but it pays to be a United States Ambassador.

As they were seated Jenny said, "You're not the only one that can get a table in a restaurant that's full."

"I heard this one time and I think this is a perfect time to repeat it. I'm not positive what it means, but," "**Touche**!"

"You don't know what that means?"

"I think it's a hairpiece, but I'm not sure."

Jenny was taking a sip when Peter said that, and her drink almost came out of her nose she laughed so hard."

Ain't love grand.

They had a delicious meal, oysters on the half shell for an appetizer, broiled lobster for the main course, and chocolate mousse for dessert. They washed it all down with The Surf's famous coffee. It was a perfect meal.

The check came and Peter looked at Jenny and said, "Well?"

"Are you expecting me to pay?" she asked with a smile.

"I'll tell you what, if you can answer this question correctly, I'll pay."

"Shoot."

"OK, if you can guess how many quarters I have in my pocket. I'll pay the check AND I'll give you both of them."

Jenny laughed so hard she almost lost her breath; consequently, the people at the tables around them started laughing. You know contagious laughter. It was a trip.

She gathered herself and so did Peter, watching her laugh that hard set him off as well. He paid the bill and they left. But as they got up to leave, the woman at the next table thanked them for the laugh and asked what they were laughing at. When Jenny told her, the woman started laughing again. It was a great time.

Peter was becoming Peter again. But no matter how you cut it, he was still The Man.

They left the restaurant and simply took a stroll around the Harbor. It was perfect.

"Isn't this place beautiful?" she said.

"Yes, you are."

"Peter!"

"No, I mean it Jenny. You take my breath away."

"You don't have to ply me with lines, although every girl likes to hear things like that, Thank you."

"You think that's a line."

"Well?"

"No way. When I say stuff, I am always right. As a matter of fact, I've only been wrong one time in my entire life."

"Oh yeah, what was that?"

"Well, one time I thought I was wrong about something. BUT I WASN'T."

"Will you stop making me laugh and get serious?"

"I am serious. Serious about you."

"Awe, just for that, I have a feeling you're going to get lucky tonight."

"Not tonight honey, I have a headache."

She laughed again. "Stop, I'm getting a stomachache."

"OK. Serious. I do have to talk to you about an idea I came up with to make some money for the Children's Hospital. It involves you. That's the other reason I came."

"What can I do?"

"Bob and I were talking about an auction item which would consist of an all-inclusive couples' vacation for let's say 4 days to Washington D.C."

"Explain?"

"OK, a 4-day guided tour of the City with the tour guide being the United States Ambassador to the Soviet Union. Is that doable?"

"I don't know if I'm allowed to do that. I have to say I'm not sure."

"Can you ask? We think we can sell maybe nearly a busload as an auction item. We figure the trip for two, all-inclusive of course, would go anywhere from 10 to 25K. That's a bunch of change for the Charity."

"I don't know. What would you be promising?"

"A tour of the Pentagon, the White House, and for sure the Smithsonian. I think a night around here would be great too."

"I will try and get something like that approved. It is for a wonderful cause. It just might fly. I'm not sure about the Pentagon but the White House has tours all the time. The Smithsonian and the Inner Harbor here in Baltimore is a given."

"PLUS, an added bonus for you, I'll come with them and probably so will Bob and Arlene. How's that for sweetening the pot?"

"I would love that, really. All I can say is I'll try."

"Thank you, sweetheart."

"Boy. You think big Mr. Conti."

"You have no idea."

Chapter 26

MAFIA, LLC
The Conti Story Continues

The rest of the weekend was perfect in every way. Peter truly never wanted to leave her. His life was in turmoil and he truthfully didn't know how he could change it. He tried to not think about it when they were together, but the fact that he was a Mafia Boss just doesn't go away that easy.

Jennifer made a number of phone calls over the weekend and, with a little easing of the rules, she was able to get approval. Her position was not to be used for profit but seeing as it was for such a noble cause, the Children's Hospital following in the footsteps of the Amazing Shiners Hospital, she got the OK.

She was scheduled back in D.C. from her Russian tour around the first part of December and would be there through new years. That's kind of a slow time for our government because everyone is anxious to get home around the Christmas break. That gave Peter and Bob actual dates they could work from for the auction item. It was set. For Peter the only problem was that was months away. He did not want to be separated from Jenny that length of time. When he departed, the two of them felt lost. He got on the plane with a heavy heart.

Peter called Bob Sunday night when he got home and gave him the good news. Bob asked Peter if he had time in the morning to meet with

Mrs. Marlo so she could make some calls to research airfare and accommodations. Bob then said, "Wait, let's do lunch and talk about it first. We can both fill her in when we get back. Is that OK with you?"

"Wait, I spoke too soon are you trying to trick me into another free lunch?"

"Nope. Let's just eat across the street from my office at Marley's. I'm buying."

"About time."

They both laughed.

"Noon?" suggested Bob.

"See you there Mr. Mayor."

The lunch went perfectly. The Mayor was happy with everything that had been discussed. He had his secretary Mary check into all of the details, and all went well. The auction item was a done deal.

Peter's life was complicated, but he was working on uncomplicating it. He still didn't know how he was going to do it. All he knew was that he wanted his life to revolve around Jennifer Taylor Grier.

The next month or so Peter stayed away from the Delaware Grill. He talked with Tony Sotto constantly reaffirming that Tony was running things and that he was just an overseer. That was starting to be established in Sotto's mind, but Tony kept wondering what Peter was up to.

Peter was easing his way out, but that isn't easy. People in that line of work don't particularly get to walk away. They know too much. The usual way they got out was not what Peter had in mind, that's for sure. He kept at Tony reassuring him that his role was the business side and he had pretty much covered that aspect. Peter was aware that what he wanted was going to take time. Time, he didn't want to spend. He thought by staying away he could revive the old adage out of sight out of mind. He hoped it was working.

It was working in one aspect because Alexander Turskin had been following Peter for almost a week now. He was doing the research his boss Igor Teriseko had asked him to do. Find out who ran the operation, Tony Sotto or Peter Conti. He gathered that Conti must be an intricate part but noted that Sotto ran the operation. He concluded his fact gathering and was ready to go back to Russia to report. The only thing left on his plate was to break Conti's neck. He was told to twist it almost off, just like he did to Anton Chekov, and to take pictures. Last but not least, leave a note on Conti's body warning Sotto and his crew, **the Russians are back.**

Peter left the restaurant to head home to his office there. As he left, he had a strange feeling. Like he was being followed. He watched behind as he drove and noticed a black Chevy Impala was definitely following him. He didn't think cop. They had no reason. He suspected Russians.

That night Peter slept in a chair in the corner of his bedroom. He had placed pillows in his bed to act like it was his body laying there. Turned out to be the smartest thing he ever did.

Just after midnight he heard the stair creek, his warning sign. He was alerted immediately. He stayed motionless in the unlit corner. A person dressed all in black crept into Peter's room and slid over to the side of the bed. He had a gun pointed at the lump under the covers and said with a Russian accent, "Wake up you piece of shit Igor Terisenko sends his regards."

Peter answered from the corner of the room, "I am awake." And put two holes in the man's back and one in his head.

Blood was every ware. Peter immediately called Tony, told him what happened and told him to get over there and bring a cleaner with him. (A cleaner is someone that takes care of bodies and the crime scene, just like nothing had happened.)

Luckily Hazel was spending the night with a sick friend or Peter would have had a lot of explaining to do. This way, after the body was taken care of and the mess cleaned up, no one was the wiser.

"What the fuck Boss. Who was this guy?"

"I'm afraid the Russians are too stupid to heed a warning and this time there's nobody we can send back. I don't want to be fucking around with a dead body. Double bury this son of a bitch and give me some time to think. This can't go on."

Double burying is just that. You stick the guy in a coffin underneath another deceased person, right in the same coffin just below in another compartment. They got a funeral home on their payroll for that. The trick is you need strong pallbearers. Once the coffin is in the ground, it's over. No body, no crime.

"What are we going to do about this? Should we put the spies out again Boss?"

"Yes, we have to, but I think this guy was here alone, probably for two reasons. One, just doing reconnaissance to gather as much info as he can and get it back to Russia so Terisenko can evaluate their position and their chances before even thinking of making a move. Two, to kill me, probably to retaliate for killing the first motherfucker he sent. You know, the one whose neck I broke. I'm getting tired of this shit Tony. Let me work out a few things. This Russian shit has got to be taken care of one way or another."

"Whatever you say Boss."

"I'm thinking about something. But I need to go out of town a few days to work out some details before I say anything. It's just an idea. I need to check something out first. Just keep taking care of things. Hell, you've been doing that all along anyway."

Peter knew that, in order for him to hand the reins over to Sotto, two things had to happen. First, he needed to make some kind of a deal with Tony Sotto because you can't just say I quit. And second, Igor

Terisenko and probably the number two man in Russia had to die. That would end the Russian threat for sure. No way they would try anything over here again. They had too much collateral damage already. They don't need the business that bad. Not if they think they started something that would bring the Italians to their country. And the murder of Terisenko and his right-hand man would put an exclamation mark on that. The Italians already killed an entire crew of theirs. They also lost the hit men Terisenko sent, and then hopefully Terisenko himself will be killed in the near future. The next guy's not going to want to take that kind of a chance. If he can work a deal with Sotto, that takes the Russians out of play, he could claim he's done all he wanted to accomplish and fulfilled Vito's legacy. He'll claim that that's the only reason he became the Godfather. He'd be done and Tony Sotto would get what was rightfully his in the first place. He would be the head of the family. He would be the Godfather. As far as the Russians, it would cement the fact that it would be smart for them to just leave well enough alone. They do business there and the Italians do business here. The war would be over.

For Peter, it was a way out. With the Russians gone, his life would no longer be in jeopardy. The hit would be off. Peter realized that for him to pull this off, he had to go to Russia and take care of business. That would be the deal he would make with Sotto. Peter would "off" the Russian bosses alone. Thus, giving Sotto and his men free rein to do business with no interference from the Russians. He'd do it alone. It would be his final act as the Godfather. When he was through. He was through.

Peter wanted a fresh start with Jenny at his side. Jackie would never leave his heart. He would love her until the day he died but God left him room in his heart to let another person in. Peter would do whatever he had to, to make that happen, even if he died trying. In order for that to happen, Peter had to do two things he really didn't want to do; one, use Jenny as a source for him to enter Russia and, two, get outside help.

He was desperate and desperate times lead to desperate measures. There are four men in Peter's life that would die for one another; no matter what and no matter when. For Peter, this was that time. These guys are killing machines. They're Special Forces Green Berets and Peter was about to call out for help.

Chapter 27

MAFIA, LLC
The Conti Story Continues

"Orin, it's Peter."

Major Orin Olsen was Special Forces Green Beret and the leader of the five-man Green Beret stealth unit that Peter, along with Nigel (Nitro) Burk, Joseph (The Cat) LaVaca, and Thomas (William Tell) Tully, were part of in Vietnam. These men saved each other's lives so many times you couldn't count them on two hands. They were brothers in arms and there wasn't anything that they wouldn't do for one another. Captain Olsen, now Major Olsen has been stationed at Fort Bragg, North Carolina and is the head of Intelligence there.

"Peter, you are not going to believe me, but I was minutes from picking up the phone and calling you. Great minds think alike."

"You were, is something wrong?"

"Not at all. I was calling to tell you that Nitro is stateside. He's got some leave time, so he's stopping here at Bragg this weekend. I was calling to see if you wanted to join us."

"Hell, yes. When is he getting there?"

"Friday afternoon. He's coming in on a transport that's due to arrive at 1400 hours. I'll grab him when it lands."

"I'll be there, and I'll be with you when you do. I miss you guys."

"Terrific! Did you just call out of thin air?"

"Not really Orin. You know the trouble I got in when I was hell bent on revenge?"

"Peter, of course. I'm still sick over what happened. Did the information I provided help?"

"That and then some. I got my revenge, but it turned out to be much more involved then I thought."

"Are you in a lot of trouble?"

"I'll explain when we get together. I don't want to talk about it over the phone. But if you can, I need a little more Intel on another Russian guy."

"Peter, what the fuck have you gotten yourself into?"

"More than you can ever imagine but with this information I think I can get myself out. Lock, Stock, and Barrel."

"What do you need?"

"I need everything you can get on a guy named Igor Terisenko. He's the head of the Russian Syndicate in Moscow. Everything your Intelligence Department has on him. We'll talk when I come there. Make me a room reservation near you for Thursday night."

"Jesus Christ, the head of the Russian Mob, in Russia. What the fuck Peter? Jesus Christ, God All Mighty pal. OK, I understand, you know I'll get you whatever you need. That goes without saying. You know that. And yeah, of course, I'll absolutely get you a place near me. You'll be in the bedroom next to mine you asshole. Call me with your itinerary and I'll pick you up at the airport. It will be good to see you buddy."

"Thanks Orin. I'm anxious to see you and Betty both and seeing Nitro, what a bonus."

"Peter, if you need anything else, Jesus I can't believe I'm saying this, but I mean anything, I'm here for you."

"Just the Intel Orin, see you Thursday."

Part one is taken care of. Orin has his pulse on information throughout the world. He'll have what Peter needs. Now for the hard part for Peter. That is, not hard for Jenny, but for him to involve her in the slightest of ways was something he dreaded. In reality, all he was using her for was a reason to go to Russia so he could acquire a visa. He wanted everything to be legal when she was involved, or he could get forged documents easy as pie. She really wasn't involved in anything else at all. He was going to call her and say he wanted to come to Russia to see her and that he missed her. The fact is, he did. He had to wait to call because he needed the Intel from Orin before he could make a specific date. The visa would be nothing but a formality. His plan was to fly into Moscow, do what he had to do, as quickly as possible, and then on to St. Petersburg, like he just had a layover in Moscow.

His plan was in the works. Now he needed to make a deal with Tony Sotto.

Peter walked into his old office, now occupied by Tony Sotto, and confronted Tony right off the bat. No sense in taking his plan any further if Tony wasn't on board.

"Tony, we need to talk."

"What's up Boss?"
"That's just it. In reality Tony, you're the boss and have been ever since Vito died. All I've done is bring business ideas, but you're the

guy who has implemented all of them. I don't deserve the honor of being called Godfather,"

"Bullshit. You're the leader."

"No Tony, the men listen to me because of business, and yeah maybe this all happened because of The Flower Man. But he's gone. I'm Peter Conti, not The Flower Man."

"What are you saying Peter?"

"I'm saying you're the rightful heir to Vito's throne, and I have a plan to put you where you belong. I never wanted this. I'm glad my business sense made a lot more money for everyone, but I've done all I can. You're the one that makes it work. I know I can't just say I want out and it's done. The other families might not go for that but if I earn my way out, that's another story. Here's what I propose: You tell anybody who asks that I came to you and wanted out. You tell them you said it don't work that way. Then I came up with a deal. Here's the deal the Russians are coming back. A war is brewing like no war we've ever had. Business and lives will be lost. I will personally end that from happening. I'll finish my revenge and end the Russian threat. In return, I'm out and you're in."

"How you plan on doing that?"

"I'll cut off the head of the snake in Russia. I'll go to Russia and take out their leadership. I've already killed Terski, now I'll kill Terisenko and whoever else needs to go. Whoever is left will not want to fuck with us for any reason anymore. Win. Win. The organization keeps it all and they get the Godfather they deserve, you."

"Look, I understand where you're coming from. I like it of course. I've been waiting in the wings for a long time. You sure about this?"

"Never wanted this. Only wanted to revenge my wife. Let me do this for Vito, and you, and the whole crew. But mainly for me, I want out."

"Maybe this can be pulled off, but I am definitely going to hear the words, you know too much."

"True, but you know enough about me to put me in the electric chair, for Christ's sake. That's a standoff that both sides win. I'm sworn to secrecy and so is everyone else. I'll just drift away like smoke. You're already in position here in the office. The guys haven't even seen me in a long time. They've been taking their orders from you. Nothing will change. The only change will be that I'll wipe out the competition and leave it all to you. I'll get in touch with you when the deed is done. You're a good man, Tony. I mean you're a good man, Godfather. We got a deal?"

The two men shook hands and Tony said, "DEAL!"

Chapter 28

MAFIA, LLC
The Conti Story Continues

Major Orin Olsen was all smiles when he saw his friend walking off the plane.

"Hello Peter," he said as he hugged his friend.

"It's been too long my friend."

"Let's get a beer. Not here, there's a gin joint around the corner from the house. We can stop there. Or are you too high and mighty to drink beer now?"

"Kiss my ass. I'll suck beer off the bar rag, if necessary."

Both guys laughed and headed out.

Orin started the conversation with, "I kind of don't know how to ask this, but how did the information I gathered for you last time work out. Don't be specific?"

"I avenged Jackie, but it didn't really help."

"Well I didn't hear from you and I was worried, but I was able to check things out through the Intelligence grapevine. What we got was that an unknown assailant who they were calling The Flower Man wiped out the entire Russian Syndicate in New York. They are saying single-handedly."

"I heard that. But like I said, it didn't really help, Jackie was still gone."

"I don't need to know anymore. I still feel your pain. What have you been doing since?"

"That's what I'm doing here. Through a series of coincidences, I got involved in the, don't get upset, the Flower Man got involved, in the Mafia."

"WHAT THE FUCK!"

"I know Orin. But I'm ok. The law has not even knocked on my door. But I want out."

"Jesus Christ Peter. I don't think I can help you or at least I don't know how?"

"The information on Terisenko is key."

"How?"

"The guy put a contract out on me. They tried to kill me twice now, right in my home. I killed the guys they sent, but it's only a matter of time. I need to go to Russia and kill that motherfucker before he kills me."

"This ain't Nam Peter. Jesus Christ."

"Maybe not, but it's still a war and I'm in the middle of it."

"I can get you the Intel on the son of a bitch, but I can't do much more. I can't get you over there or nothing even close. Maybe Italy or

France. We got transports going over there all the time, but I can't get you in Russia, no way no how."

"Don't need you to. I just need to know the where abouts of Terisenko and what his movement pattern is. Can you get me that? If he has a right-hand man, that too."

"Motherfucker," said Orin.

"You know how many times you've said motherfucker, and Jesus Christ, and God All Mighty, in the last fifteen minutes?"

"Jesus Christ, I can't believe you've been counting."

Both men laughed. It wasn't a laughing matter, but they had been through so much together. Death and killing just came naturally. Probably killed a couple of hundred guys over there. War is hell and they lived it, together, along with three other guys. One more of them was on his way there for a nice reunion tomorrow.

"Don't say anything to Nitro. No reason to get him involved," said Peter.

"Bullshit, maybe he can help. We will be a team as long as the last one of us is breathing."

"No Orin. I'm sorry I've got you involved."

"Shut your face. Someone is trying to kill you. We're in. Now drink your drink. Betty told me to bring you right home. She'll kick my ass if we don't get there soon."

"Oh shit, why didn't you say that sooner? Let's go. She'll kick my ass too."

Peter walked in the door to a big hug and kiss.

"Peter, I haven't seen you since the tragedy. I have no words. Jackie was such a wonderful person. We are both broken-hearted for you."

"Thank you, Betty. Jackie thought of you like a sister."

"You know, I was in the hospital with some minor surgery when it all happened. Orin told you, didn't he?"

"Of course, Betty. You didn't have to say that. I got your letter. Thank you. It was beautiful."

"I'm just glad to see you now. You look wonderful Peter. Of course, you've always been soo damn handsome anyway."

"Betty, I'm standing right here for crying out loud," said Orin with a smile.

"Be quiet, you always said you thought he was handsome too."

"Peter, that's a lie. I said I thought you were nice looking. That's different."

Peter laughed out loud and hugged Betty again.

"Tell us what you've been doing all this time," asked Betty.

"I'll tell you over dinner. Pick the best place in town. I'm treating. I'm with two of my favorite people in the whole world and I want to celebrate."

"Well, I'm not going dressed like this."

"Why you look beautiful," said Peter.

"Bull, I can see you learned a lot from Orin cause your sounding just like him."

"Thanks for the compliment. Go change if you want. The sky's the limit tonight. Oh, by the way, have I mentioned I'm rich?"

"WHAT," said Orin?

"I'll tell you all about it at dinner. Right now, point me to the restroom."

Orin just stared at Peter for the first five minutes at Dominic's, the best steakhouse Fayetteville, North Carolina had to offer. It's pricey, but Peter insisted.

"OK, spit it out. I've been waiting patiently for you to follow up on your by the way I'm rich comment."

"I don't know how this happened, but when I was a kid in college, I met a very nice man. We befriended one another. He was an Italian man who was born very close to where my family is from in Italy. He told me stories about the old country and I just enjoyed his company. Pass the bread will you Cap?"

"Don't you dare leave us hanging and I'm a Major now Sergeant, if you don't mind."

"I'm just getting a piece of bread, jeez."

"Will you let him finish Orin, jeez?"

All three laughed.

"Well as I was about to say. He was very rich, and he died, and he left me everything. Could you pass the butter now?"

"Wait, wait, just a Goddamn minute. That's it?"

"Yeah."

"How rich?"

"A magnificent mansion where I live there now. He also left me a half dozen really beautiful cars, and a whole bunch of money and investments. Oh yeah and a restaurant too. I'm hungry, are you guys hungry?"

"Holy mother of God! You're paying tonight," said Orin.

"Shut up, I told you I was."

"Congratulations Peter. It couldn't happen to a nicer guy," injected Betty.

"Thank you, Betty. He was always wonderful to me, seems like forever. He was never married, and he told me I was the son he never had. I was heartbroken when he died."

"I'll bet you were," she added sympathetically.

Orin then said, "Why couldn't you say it like that to me. Now I feel bad."

"I did that on purpose. Just to piss you off."

"Well it worked. Congratulations. Are you using all those cars? I'm just saying."

They all laughed again.

They had a wonderful meal. You could tell from a hundred yards away how close these two men were to one another. A bond like no other is forged when men fight side by side, saving each other's life numerous times. It's hard to explain. But it lasts a lifetime.

The next day the two friends stood next to the runway waiting for the third man of their five-man stealth force to land. Nigel (Nitro) Burke got off the plane with a smile you could hang your coat on. They hugged each other, very unmilitary like. None of them seemed to care.

"Jesus Peter, you look like a Goddamn movie star. Did you have a facelift or something?"

"Yeah, and I had my dick lengthened too. You want to see?"

All three laughed.

They were in a bar within 15 minutes.

"Where you stationed now Nitro," asked Peter.

"I'm in Germany. I hate it there. There's nothing to blow up."

They all laughed again.

"What about you Peter? How you been doing after, you know?"

"I'll never forget her. I came to realize that, even though it's been awhile now, I'm doing well. My business life has been good, and I've come into some money so, all in all, I'm good."

Orin cut in, "He's fucking rich. The son of a bitch."

"Rich!"

"Shit happens," replied Peter.

Orin got serious for a moment and added, "Nitro, he got himself in some big-time trouble."

"Orin, Jesus Christ. I didn't want Nitro to get involved."

"Involved in what. What happened? You need my help?"

"Peter, if one of us is in trouble, we all are. Maybe Nitro can help. Maybe he has a way of getting you into Russia. That's all I'm saying," said Orin as serious as a heart attack.

"Russia, Russia, what the fuck are you talking about?"

"OK, but this goes without saying. This has to be between us. Period."

"Shut the fuck up. Who do you think you're talking to?"

"I know Nigel, but this is some bad shit. I think you know the story of how Jackie was killed."

"Of course, Peter. I was overseas or you know, when."

"Stop, of course I know. Well the Russian bastard that machine gunned that Bagel place and took my Jackie from me was in the Russian Mob. Bottom line, I took him and the rest of those pieces of shit out. All of them and I got away with it."

"Good fucking deal. I hope you made them suffer."

"Well, the main man who runs the organization from Russia has put a hit out on me. I've killed the first two guys who tried so far, but I'm sick of looking over my shoulder. I plan on going over there and taking out this guy and whoever else I need to, first. How's that for a holy shit?"

"Holy shit."

"Right," added Orin.

Nitro added, "So you need us to go over there with you to kill a bunch of guys. That ain't going to be easy Peter."

"No, Nigel. I don't want you involved anymore than even knowing this shit. I just needed Intel from Cap; I mean the Major. And, as far as getting in, I have an in."

"Who, what, how?"

"Jesus, that's a lot of questions for three words. But anyway, here it is. I met someone. I never thought in a million years there could be anyone else in my life, but this woman is something special."

"Good for you buddy. Tell us more," said Orin.

"Well, I'm involved in this charity to raise money for this Children's Hospital. It's a great cause and it makes me feel good. The Mayor, who I've become friends with, brought a big-time politician in to help. She's a United States Ambassador. We hit it off and it has become serious, very serious."

"That's wonderful," said Nigel.

"That's where the "in" comes from. As much as I don't want to get her involved and I mean in the least, she's my into Russia. She's the U.S. Ambassador to the Soviet Union. I can get a visa to visit her, take those cocksuckers out, and I'm free and clear and all of a sudden, I'm Peter again. I think I can start a new life with her. I can't believe I'm saying this, but I really love this woman guys,"

"Jesus Christ Almighty, is there anything else that's happened to you cause this is starting to get wild?" said Orin shaking his head as he said it.

"Yes, but that's not important. What is somewhat important is this. I haven't been able to figure out a way to get a weapon over there. I'd love an assault rifle, but HOW?"

Orin interjected, "I can't help you their pal. Don't know what to tell you."

"I do," said Nitro. "Fuck shooting them. Blow the motherfuckers up."

"Yeah, I'll just bring a couple of sticks of dynamite on the plane with me."

"What the fuck, you know who you're talking to. I'll fix you up a solution that fits in a toothpaste tube. Stick a detonator in a small box of fuses cause it looks like one. You can stick that right in your luggage and then all you need is a pager. You stick it under their car, call the pager, it blows, no collateral damage and you're out of there with no one the wiser. They try and kill a friend of mine and this is what they get. What do you think?"

"Perfect. But do you guys know what you're getting yourselves into?"

In unison they said, "Go fuck yourself."

Chapter 29

MAFIA, LLC
The Conti Story Continues

Peter left Fayetteville with three things. From Orin, the Intel on Igor Teriseko, which included addresses of where he lived, where his office was, where he had lunch every day, and who his right-hand man is. Orin had included pictures of Terisenko and of Yuri Mantanko, the next in line and pictures of Terisenko's office and his home. From Nitro, he got an emptied-out tube of toothpaste that was then filled with enough explosives to blow a car to smithereens. It was safe to transport because it needed a detonator in order to blow. Plus, he could carry it right in his toiletry kit. Thirdly, he left knowing that he had two guys that would walk into hell with him no matter the reason. This was starting to look possible.

Next, was the hard thing for Peter.

"Jenny, hi it's Peter."

"Hi, oh my God it's good to hear your voice. I'm so happy you called."

"I had to. I miss you too much."

"Me too. But it's only 9 weeks and we'll see each other. But who's counting?"

"Well. I can't wait 9 weeks. Any chance you can get some time off over there. It's only a 17-hour flight. I can do that standing on my head."

"God yes. Oh Peter, I love you. You know that right? Oh no, here it comes, I can feel it."

"Ditto." He said jokingly and continued with, "There I said it, I didn't want to disappoint you. But I really do love you too Jenny."

"When can you come?"

"ASAP. But I think I need a visa."

"Yes, you do, but I'll take care of that. Just fax me over a copy of your passport. All the information I need is on that. I can get you a visa in a day or two."

"Fantastic. I'll book a flight as soon as I can. I'm not kidding. I am missing the hell out of you."

"I can't wait sweetheart. This is the best call I've gotten in a long time."

"Give me the number to fax it to and I'll see you before you know it."

"Bye sweetheart, I love you. I said it first this time," said Peter.

"Jenny answered with, "Ditto."

Peter hung up the phone with the biggest mixed emotions he had ever had. He wanted to see this woman, that was never truer, but he felt like he used her. It was maddening to him. Peter realized what he was doing was for the two of them and it had to be done. He wanted to make it up to her but didn't know how. Then it struck him.

"Mom."

"Hi Peter, I'm so happy to see you, come on in."

"Mom, I need to talk to you."

"Oh Oh."

"No Mom it's not bad. It might even be good, but I'm so conflicted."

"What's the matter sweetheart?"

"Mom, I love Jackie. I do now and I always will."

"I know that son, everybody does. What's wrong?"

"Nothings wrong Mom. But Jenny, I can't get her out of my mind."

"That's a good thing Peter."

"I know Mom. Here's the thing. I think I love her."

"You think?"

"No Mom, I know I love her and I want to be with her."

"Again sweetheart, that's a good thing."

"Yes Mom, I know. The thing is I want to be with her forever. I want to ask her to marry me. But Jackie?"

"Oh, dear God. Peter let me ask you this. If it were you who were gone, would you want Jackie to be alone for the rest of her life? Wouldn't you want her to find happiness or would you want her to just mourn forever?"

"I love you Mom."

"I love you too Peter, but I think it's Jenny you need to say that to."

"I'm going to Russia. The trip's all set. I think I want to bring a ring."

"This is wonderful news Peter, wonderful."

"Don't say anything to anyone Mom. We haven't been together all that long. She might say NO."

"Peter, I saw the way that woman looked at you. She won't say no. I guarantee you she won't."

"I hope so Mom."

"Mothers are never wrong."

Peter booked the perfect flight to St. Petersburg. There was a 14-hour layover in Moscow. He couldn't have asked for a better flight. His next stop was to the family jewelers. Peter bought a very nice diamond ring, not gaudy but not small. He bought what he thought Jenny would like. All he thought about was Jenny. The Russian scumbag that was trying to kill him was almost a second thought to him.

If Peter was honest with himself, he would of preferred not to do what he had to do, but like any war, you fight and kill to protect. Peter was protecting Tony Sotto and the men plain and simple. There was definitely going to be a war and many of those guys would die. But, the true bottom-line for Peter was, it was either Terisenko, or him.

Chapter 30

MAFIA, LLC
The Conti Story Continues

Peter's plane touched down at 6:45AM Moscow time. His connecting flight to St. Petersburg wasn't until 9:00 PM. He had plenty of time, but no time to waste. He only had carried on luggage so there was no waiting for bags. He had no problem in customs and, before you knew it, he was standing outside of SVO Sheremetyevo International Airport, the busiest airport in all of Russia, trying to flag down a cab.

He waved one down and just said, "Lenin's Mausoleum."

Lenin's Mausoleum is situated in the heart of Red Square, the height of American tourism. The Museum is the final resting place of communist revolutionary Vladimir Lenin. Peter knew he could get lost in that crowd. Teriseko's office was just on the edge of what is called Red Square, so Peter felt safe taking a cab. An American going to Red Square is absolutely commonplace.

Donned in a mustache, sunglasses, and a baseball cap he strolled in the direction he had marked on the makeshift map he got from Orin. He also had a picture of the office. Peter didn't want to guess where Teriseko would go for lunch, so he decided to light him up like a Roman candle right in front of his office. A shinny new black limousine pulled in and parked in the allyway next to the office. Igor

Teriseko and Yuri Mantanko, who was driving, departed the vehicle and headed to a back door that was easy access from the limo.

Peter waited a short while to let them settle into whatever they were going to do inside. He knew they would come out for lunch at some point, so he was golden. He drifted over to the back of the limo and, pretending to tie his shoe, inserted the toothpaste tube bomb loaded with a detonator and a pager taped on in between the frame and the gas tank of the gagster limo. It took but seconds to do that.

From there he dropped a letter in a nearby mailbox addressed to whom it may concern with Terisenko's office's address on it. It was a warning and the last warning the Russians were going to get. They weren't that stupid. This was enough warning to keep them in Russia. He then meandered over to a bench that had a perfect view of the parked vehicle and was situated right next to a phone booth and he waited. It was 11:10AM Moscow time. At exactly 1:00PM Terisenko and Mantanko exited the building and jumped in the limo. Orin's information is that he went to lunch around then everyday. Orin was right. Mantanko started up the limo and Peter called the pager. **BOOM** the blast rocked both the buildings that the limo sat between, but no damage to either of the buildings.

Teriseko and Mantango were no more. Good riddance. Peter was free. Peter watched with the other tourists for a little while. He didn't want to be seen as the only person leaving the crime scene. When a few other people started to leave, so did he. He walked a short distance to the other side of the Square, grabbed a cab back to the airport, and waited.

He had lunch and made a vulgar pass at the waitress. He wanted to be noticed. He did the same thing at a different restaurant in the airport at dinner. Again, an alibi, of which he knew he didn't need. This was all just in case and all for Jenny.

He called her at about 2:00 PM and told her he was in. She was mad that she couldn't get the day off because of work meetings. She would have liked to drive the 7 hours to Moscow to meet his plane. He told her to hold her horses. He would be there before midnight. She was elated.

He landed at 11:20 PM St. Petersburg time. Jenny's smile lit up the entire gate. She waved and yelled, "Peter, Peter, I'm over here."

"You look more beautiful every time I see you."

He barely got words out of his mouth when Jenny just grabbed him and gave him a kiss that was so passionate that words can't do it justice.

The two had an aura around them that could only be described by the word LOVE.

Peter couldn't take his eyes off of her. She was like an angel. She gripped his hand in such a way that it would take a crowbar to dislodge it. They went for a drink at the only bar that was still open and was near Jenny's apartment. They both couldn't wait to hold each other in their arms, but they just wanted to talk first.

"Peter how could this possibly be? We've known each other for such a short time."

"I felt this way towards you the first time we met with Bob for lunch. Jenny, I swear I really didn't want to. I told myself that the moment I saw you, but I couldn't help it. You are beautiful inside and out. You killed me right there. I tried to be cool, but I know I failed."

"Bob told me that I was really going to like you. He built you up so big I just knew you were going to look like Danny DiVito from that TV show Taxi, then I saw you."

Peter actually burst out laughing.

"Plus, I couldn't believe it, you actually made a move on me. Guys do not make moves on me. You did, and here we are. The crazy thing is, I'm 15 minutes from ripping your clothes off."

"I'm not a plaything you know," Peter said almost laughing and they kissed right there in the bar. They left their drinks.

The next morning, they woke up early but didn't get out of bed for a little while. As a matter of fact, it was quite awhile. They showered and went across the street to a little bakery that served breakfast.

"When we're finished. How about you show me your town. I am a tourist you know."

"What are you interested in? Besides me," she said with a giant smile.

"Well, for sure, the Winter Palace of Peter the First also known as Peter the Great. That makes sense doesn't it?"

Jenny laughed but said yes it does. "OK we'll start there. Then where?"

"You're the guide?"

"I think St. Isaac's Cathedral is magnificent."

"OK we'll go there next."

They had a beautiful day. The night was magical. Peter had the ring ready, but he was going to wait for the right moment. He was petrified that she might say no.

They took the two-day bus tour and Jenny saw St. Petersburg like she had never seen it before. She worked most of the time, so sightseeing was not on her schedule.

There were only two days left before Peter was going home. Everything was perfect so far. The news announced that two known members of the Russian Syndicate were car bombed in Moscow by a feuding competitor. No mention of America. But first things first, Peter called Tony Sotto.

"Tony the war is over. Terisenko and their number two guy, Yuri Mantanko are dead. I left a warning for the next guy, as if their deaths weren't warning enough, that said: we can find you anywhere, stay out of America and we'll stay out of Russia, I signed it The Flower Man. It's done."

"Good news Conti. I knew you would take care of this. The boys and me talked over what we discussed. You did everything you said you would do. We're making a lot of money over here and now the Russians are out, no competition. We are all sworn to secrecy and The Flower Man is dead. Thank you, Peter, **You're out.**"

"Wait Tony, one last thing. In the bottom left drawer of the desk, there's the deed to the Delaware Grill. I signed it and made it out to you. It's a gift from me to you for all you've done for me. Thank you, Godfather and goodbye."

He did it. He was out. One thing down, now for the second, and he was scared.

That evening Peter and Jenny were walking along the Moika Embankment, a stoic walking area in the City headed to the bronze horseman's statue of Peter the Great, the founder of the City. They sat on a bench admiring the beautiful statue when all of a sudden Peter said, "Jenny, you have changed my life."

"Both of our lives have been changed."

"Let me finish, I know we haven't known each other all that long and I know you love your job."

He continued with, "But do you think it would be possible to just leave everything behind? I mean everything. Here's the thing, I bought a beautiful Villa on the Amalfi Coast. It's magnificent. What I'm saying is, I love you Jenny!" Peter reached into his pocket for the ring and said, "Jennifer Taylor Grier, Will YOU BE MY WIFE?"

Jenny looked down at the beautiful ring and hesitated for a second. She had been waiting for this moment her entire life. The right man just never came along and now he has. She started to cry. They were happy tears, tears of joy. She took a deep breath, looked up at Peter, and just said, "**YES**."

THE END
(Maybe?)

Made in the USA
Monee, IL
14 January 2020